BLESS YOUR BONES, SAMMY

Frances Fitzpatrick Wright

drawings by Steele Savage

ABINGDON PRESS

Nashville   *New York*

BLESS YOUR BONES, SAMMY is based largely on, and adapted from, the author's series of stories which first appeared in "Boys and Girls." The story from which the first chapter is adapted appeared originally in "The Southern Agriculturist."

For
Robert Dickerson
to whom books are bread

CONTENTS

One for the Money,
Two for the Show

SOME PEOPLE COULD LOSE TWO DOLLARS, AND they would never miss it. But not Samuel Thaxton Milliken, Jr. Two dollars was all the money he had in this world, and he had saved it up to spend at the circus.

The first Sammy Thax knew of the circus coming was when he went to Richfield, the first Saturday in June, with his father. On the side of Smith's Livery Stable he saw a large, brightly colored sign that said: COMING JULY 4TH, 1904, BARNUM AND BAILEY'S WORLD RENOWNED CIRCUS. The sign was decorated with pictures of beautiful ladies in spangled, pink skirts, short and fluffy, standing on the backs of galloping horses. There were also pictures of clowns and elephants and snarling lions in fancy cages. Sammy Thax had never seen the like. "Just look a'yonder, Pa," he said, pointing to the sign. "A circus is comin' the fourth of July. Can we come and see it?"

"I'll be in wheat threshing about then," Mr. Milliken said, "but nothing's to hinder you from coming, if you can earn the money to pay your way."

Sammy Thax breathed hard with excitement. Riding home that day, seated on the high wagon seat beside his father, Sammy Thax made up his mind to see that circus. He would earn two dollars before the fourth of July, or die trying. A half-fare ticket, the sign said, would be thirty-five cents. Then he would need some nickels for popcorn and peanuts and lemonade. He had eaten those treats at the county fair. A circus, he thought, would be sort of like the fair, but a lot more exciting. He might even have his fortune told or ride on an elephant. Rindy had done both those things once. Rindy was the hired man.

The next day was Sunday, but early Monday morning Sammy Thax set out to make himself some circus money. He walked to the neighboring farm where Mr. Will Sumpter lived and got a job worming tobacco. Sammy worked hard, going up and down the long rows, picking off the fat, ugly worms, and dropping them in a can of coal oil. He worked all day long, and about dark Mr. Sumpter said, "Time to knock off, Sam. You done me an honest day's work and better than most boys your age would'a done." Fishing from his pocket a small leather pouch, he opened it and took out a quarter, a dime, and a nickel. Sammy Thax thanked him, pocketed his money, and hurried home. At the gate, waiting for him, was his grandmother, a bent but brisk little old lady with twinkling eyes.

"I was gettin' worried about you, Sammy," she said, giving him a pat on the back. "It's plumb dark, and I reckon you are beat." Sammy Thax nodded his head, too tired even to talk to Gran.

On Tuesday Sammy Thax cleaned out the hen house for his mother, and she gave him twenty cents because he had told her he was trying to earn money for the circus. Cleaning the hen house was hot and dusty and smelly, and one nest had mites in it which came crawling over Sammy's bare arms. He took out all the straw and burned it, and soaked the nest with coal oil as his mother had told him. On Wednesday he sold a steel trap to his best friend, Jud Harkins, for fifteen cents. That made seventy-five cents in all.

"A dollar and a quarter more is all I need," Sammy Thax told Gran that night when he went across the hall to her room, to say goodnight. Jigging a bit, he chanted, "One for the money, two for the show, three to make ready, and four to *go*."

"You'll soon make it," beamed Gran. "A boy that's worth his salt can always earn some money."

But after that, for a whole week, Sammy Thax had no luck. No one would hire him. He began to worry. Then, with the circus not a week off, the thresher came to thresh his father's wheat. Sammy Thax met the big machine at the farm gate and ran along beside it until it came to a stop at the edge of the wheatfield. He yelled up to Mr. Tim Willis, who owned the thresher, "Mister Tim, can I be your water boy?"

"I guess so, mebbe," said Mr. Willis. He was a big, brawny man with a jolly face, red as a beet now from sunburn. "What are you aimin' to charge me?"

"A quarter a day," said Sammy Thax.

"Alright, you're hired," said Mr. Willis. "We can use a bucket of good fresh water right now." He drew out a big red handkerchief and mopped the sweat from his face. "Man, it's a real scorcher."

Sammy Thax ran to the house and got a three-gallon cedar bucket and a gourd dipper. He hurried down the hill to the springhouse and filled the bucket with cold water. He hustled back up the hill to the wheatfield, and Mr. Willis said, "Good for

you, Sam. Come on, men, here's some drinkin' water. I guess you all are dry as powder; I sure am." He took a dipperful of water and drained it.

The thresher crew gathered round and drank their fill. "Boy, that's sure good cold water," they told Sammy Thax as they passed the dripping dipper down the line. A dozen times that day and a dozen times the next day Sammy Thax went to the spring and toiled back up the hill with a brimming bucket of water for the men. At sundown on the second day, as they were getting ready to pull out, Mr. Willis handed Sammy Thax fifty cents. Then with a slow smile he fished out another quarter and handed it to him. "This two bits is extry because you never let the bucket get dry," he smiled.

"Gee, thank you, sir," beamed Sammy Thax.

That night, he hurried to his grandmother's room. "Look, Gran," he said proudly as he counted his money into her hand. "I wisht it was even two dollars, but this much will do me."

"Well, Sammy, you've done fine," Gran said. "And I know you are goin' to have a big time at the circus. But you watch out for pickpockets, Sammy, there'll be an awful crowd, and somebody's likely to get your money."

Sammy Thax could hardly go to sleep, he was so excited. Next morning early he went over to Jud's house, and they made plans to go to the circus. They planned to ride double on old Ned. But when Saturday morning came, Jud's younger brother came over, very early, to say that Jud couldn't go. He had had a chill in the night, and he had a sore throat and a fever. Sammy Thax was disappointed, but right after breakfast he saddled old Ned and got ready to go by himself. He decided he would bring Jud a gift from the circus.

When he was ready to go, his mother said sternly, "Mind now, Sam, you be home before dark." His older sisters, Hester and Susan, complained that he should have polished his shoes. They liked to find fault with him, Sammy thought. But at the gate Gran was waiting. Gran was always on his side. She opened the big gate for him to ride through. But Sammy Thax said, "Whoa, Ned." He looked down at his grandmother and said, "I wisht you could go too, Gran." She thrust a hand into her apron pocket and pulled out fifty cents and handed it up to him.

"Gee, Gran," said Sammy Thax, grinning broadly, "I hate to take it."

"Never mind," said Gran, "I sold two settings of turkey eggs this week. Your pa don't hold with givin' boys money to waste, but I say a boy's first time at a circus ain't a waste."

"Gran, you sure are good to me," said Sammy Thax. His face wrinkled as he leaned down and muttered, "Gran, you ain't really goin' way off to Idaho to live with Aunt Minnie, are you?"

"Looks like I might have to," said Gran with a sigh. "But don't worry about it today, Sammy Thax."

Sammy Thax nodded, but as he rode off, he kept looking back to wave at her until he rounded the big bend in the road. He urged old Ned into a lope. It was a beautiful morning, not too hot. And with money jingling in his pocket and the circus waiting for him, he couldn't worry about anything. He began to whistle.

It was a long five miles to Richfield. When he got there, he rode straight to the fairground and hitched Ned in the shade. It was getting hotter, but he didn't mind. A brisk breeze fluttered the United States flag on top of the big tent. Sammy Thax loved the smell of the hay, sawdust, and the circus animals. He watched while the circus performers got ready for the grand march. They hitched four, big, white horses to each of the fancy, gilded, big iron cages mounted on wheels, in which were lions and tigers and leopards and monkeys. He saw two bareback riders, as pretty as the pictures on the circus sign, ride by on two prancing black horses with

14

silver bridles. Following them came two big elephants, then two baby elephants, then four Shetland ponies ridden by four monkeys in red caps and jackets trimmed with gold braid. Sammy Thax's eyes were big with wonder. He wished Jud was there. Jud would never believe all he would have to tell him. He kept thinking about the story Gran often read him, his favorite story, about Noah's ark and all the animals in it.

When the parade started, Sammy Thax followed along with some other boys, keeping abreast of it all the way. The music of the calliope made the horses prance. Once a mammoth old lion let out an angry roar, and all the boys yelled.

When they returned to the fairground and it was time for the circus to begin, Sammy Thax walked up to the ticket window and said, "I want to buy a ticket."

"You can do it, Bud," the man said. He shoved a ticket under the grating. Sammy Thax reached into his pocket and froze in his tracks. His money was gone. Not even a penny was left. His heart gave a big sickening thud. Pickpockets, maybe? He felt again, frantically, and discovered a hole in the very bottom of his pocket.

"Hurry up, Bud, you are holding up the line," barked the ticket seller.

"My money is gone." stammered Sammy Thax, red to the ears. "I've done lost it."

"Too bad, Bud," said the man, taking back the ticket, "but don't stand there gaping. Get out of the way for the other folks."

Sammy Thax walked away. He stood off by himself, feeling his empty pockets, searching in the dusty grass at his feet for his money, fighting hard to keep back the tears. He could hear the band playing and see all the happy people crowding into the big tent. Everyone else had a ticket. He thought about how hard he had worked to earn his money and about the fifty cents Gran had saved for him, and he gave a big gulp and angrily brushed away some tears. The thought of going home without seeing the circus made him feel sick. "I ain't goin' home, either," he muttered.

He ran to where he saw a circus hand cutting up raw meat. "Mister," he said, "can you give me a job? I lost my ticket money."

"It's too late, son," said the man kindly. "We don't need any extra help around here now."

Sammy Thax turned back and went over to where old Ned stood fighting flies with his tail. He was so desperate that he might have tried to crawl under the tent, but earlier he had seen a policeman walking around. He leaned against the old hack berry tree to which Ned was hitched, and tears slid down his cheeks.

He was starting to unhitch Ned and start for home when he smelled tobacco smoke. He turned around and from where he stood, he saw a puff of smoke and a tiny blaze. He snatched off his cap and ran and beat out the blaze. Then he stamped on it until there was no spark left. Someone had tossed a lighted cigarette on the ground. The grass was very dry, for it hadn't rained in three weeks, and with the breeze to fan it the flame could have spread very quickly to the edge of the big tent, a few feet away.

Someone touched Sammy Thax on the shoulder and he jumped. It was the policeman. He looked fierce. "Who started that fire?" he asked.

"I don't know, sir," said Sammy Thax, scared as a rabbit. "I put it out."

"You did, huh?" said the policeman. "Come along with me, Bud." Sammy Thax wondered if he was going to be put in jail. Gran would feel disgraced. Everything had gone wrong that day. He was scared and mad and wished he had never heard of the circus. The policeman led the way to a small tent where the circus manager was stretched out on a canvas cot, fanning himself. He sat up and said, "Hello, what's the trouble?"

"No trouble, but it could'a been trouble and

plenty of it," the policeman said. "This here farm boy spotted a blaze in the grass out there. If he hadn't been quick about it, your big top might be on fire. I thought you'd like to thank him."

The man sprang to his feet, his black eyes snapping. He followed the policeman and Sammy Thax to the burned spot, no bigger than a dinner plate, still smelling of burned grass and tobacco. He gave a long, low whistle and turned around and shook hands with Sammy Thax. "You'll do, kid," he said. "But how come you ain't inside?"

"I lost my ticket money," offered Sammy Thax.

The man took a card from a wallet and scribbled something on it. He handed it to Sammy Thax. "Keep this card in your hand," he said. "Show it at the gate, at the sideshows, the popcorn stand, anywhere there's anything you want to see, or to eat, or to drink. Understand? You won't need any money."

"Gee, thank you, mister," said Sammy Thax. As he walked away, he read what the man had written: "This kid is my guest. Do him right. H.A.J."

Sammy Thax showed the card at the ticket window, and the man who had been so impatient with him before said with a deep bow, "Yessir, young man, walk right in. Reserved seat section on your right." And Sammy Thax walked in, his heart as light as a balloon, and all his troubles forgotten.

Preacher's Coming
for Sunday Dinner

AT THE SUPPER TABLE THAT NIGHT EVERYONE
asked Sammy Thax many questions about the circus.
He answered them politely enough, but he did not
mention losing his money. He was afraid he might
be lectured by his mother or father for being careless, or teased by Hester and Susan. But later, after
the rest of the family were asleep, he tiptoed across
the hall into Gran's room. Gran seemed to sleep very
little. She was sitting in her rocking chair, reading
her worn old Bible when Sammy Thax entered.

"Sit down, Sammy," she said, very low, "and
tell me some more about the circus. I had a notion
you were savin' up somethin' to tell me."

19

Sammy Thax nodded. He told Gran about his losing the money and how he felt when he reached in his pocket and it was gone. He told her about smelling smoke and discovering the little blaze and stamping it out, and how well rewarded he had been by the circus manager. Gran leaned forward to catch every word, and her face reflected first dismay, then distress for Sammy's trouble, and at last joy. She heaved a big sigh. "All's well that ends well, Sammy," she said. "But you bring me them pants tomorrow, and I'll set a new pocket in them." She rocked a minute or two and then said, "You need a wallet, Sammy, and I've got one I've been a'savin' for you till Christmas. But I ought to have give it to you this morning. It was your Grandpa's, and it's made out of calfskin and come from Pennsylvany."

She got up and went to her little walnut bureau, opened a small drawer, and took out the wallet. She unwrapped the tissue paper around it and handed it to Sammy Thax. It was a handsome wallet, well worn, but still serviceable. Sammy Thax took it and turned it over and over, and then examined it inside. "Gee, Gran," he said, "I like it. I'll take care of it. I won't never lose it."

The next morning, early, Sammy Thax went over to Jud's house. It was a mile by the road, but Sammy Thax took the shortcut across the fields. Jud was up and dressed, but he had a woolen sock soaked in smelly camphor around his neck. He and Sammy Thax sat on the steps of the back porch, and Sammy Thax repeated all he had told Gran the night before. He also told Jud about the lions and tigers and elephants, the ponies and horses, the bareback riders and clowns, the sideshows where he had seen a lion-faced boy and a lady who weighed four hundred pounds. Shyly, at last, he told him about the fortune-teller who had said he would grow up to be a United States senator and would travel to foreign lands.

"You reckon you will?" asked Jud, looking at Sammy Thax with new respect.

"Naw," scoffed Sammy. "She made it up."

"Next year I'm a'goin' to the circus," sulked Jud. "Nobody's goin' to stop me. It wouldn't a'hurt me none to go yesterday, but Ma thinks I'm still a baby." He looked around cautiously and, seeing no one, jerked the sock from around his neck and stuffed it in his overalls pocket. "My throat don't feel sore now," he said. "It's too hot to have that old sock around my neck."

"Would your Ma let you go fishin' tomorrow, do you reckon?" asked Sammy Thax. "I bet they are bitin' good down on old Bledsoe. Rindy caught a string of perch and a catfish that weighed five pounds last Saturday."

"Sure I can go," said Jud, throwing out his chest. "I'll be over to your house about seven o'clock in the mornin'."

"I'll be ready," said Sammy Thax. "I got to go now. Ma told me to hurry back."

The next morning after breakfast Sammy Thax went to the smokehouse and got out his long cane fishing pole. He went to the toolshed and got the grubbing hoe and then to the woodpile beyond the backyard gate. On the edge of the woodpile the dirt was soft, and he dug up some earthworms and dropped them into a dirty fruit jar. His mother came from the orchard with a basket of peaches. She stopped when she saw what Sammy Thax was doing. "Now, Sammy Thax, you put up that fishin' pole and come in the house," she said. "The preacher and his wife will be here for dinner tomorrow, and you've got to churn for me this mornin'."

"Aw, Ma, that's a girl's job," growled Sammy Thax. "Why can't Hester or Susan churn?"

"Hester is pickin' butterbeans, and Susan is ironin' the best tablecloth," his mother snapped.

"Gran likes to churn," protested Sammy Thax.

"Gran is bakin' a pound cake," his mother said. She wiped her hot, rosy face with her apron. "Cuttin' kindlin' is boy's work, Sam, but many is the time I've cut it because you forgot to do it. You put up that pole and them worms right now and come with me."

Reluctantly, with a long face, Sammy Thax obeyed. Old Bowser rolled his eyes at him in sympathy. He followed close behind and lay down by the back steps.

The well-scrubbed barrel churn stood in its frame on the back porch. Sammy Thax stood glumly by and watched his mother empty into it two big pans of sour milk with thick cream on top, that she had brought up from the springhouse below the orchard. She fastened down the lid and tied a long, blue-checked gingham apron around Sammy's neck.

"There now," she said cheerfully, "it's ready for you. Get to work and see how quick you can churn it. Then you can go fishin' if you want to."

Sammy Thax sat down beside the churn, grabbed the handle, and as he cranked it, the barrel turned over and over. The clabber inside made a big sloshing sound. He was miserable. He hated for the preacher and his wife to come to dinner. When they came, he had to keep his Sunday clothes on all day and mind his manners and never ask for a second helping. The house was always so primped up with flowers and doilies and the long white tablecloth, he had to be careful not to touch anything. Women, he decided, were mighty bossy people.

Bowser sneaked up the back steps and lay down near the churn with his head on both front paws. Sammy Thax's right arm began to ache. He turned the churn slower and slower. Gran appeared in the kitchen door, and he whined, "Gran, this milk is too cold. It's foamin'. It won't never come."

Gran came over and said, very low, "I don't see how it can be cold, Sammy, a warm mornin' like this. But a mite of hot water won't hurt anything, I reckon." She went into the kitchen and came back with a steaming teakettle. Carefully she unfastened the churn lid, poured in a small amount of water, and clamped the lid back on. "Now then," she said, giving Sammy Thax a pat on the shoulder, "churn right peart, and it ought to come soon."

Fiercely Sammy Thax turned the churn. He wondered why his mother was so bent on having the churning done that morning. There were two brown crocks full of yellow butter and a big jar of buttermilk in the springhouse. Hester came in from the garden with a bucket of butterbeans. Susan took the newly ironed tablecloth to the dining room and came back to help with shelling the butterbeans. They sat down facing each other at the entrance to the back hall, where it was cool, and began chattering as they shelled the beans. Sammy Thax could overhear them talking about what they would wear to church the next day, whether their beaux would be there, and giggling.

"Ma," called Sammy Thax, "make Hester or Susan finish this old churning and lemme shell beans."

His mother came out of the kitchen with a plump, half-picked frying chicken in her hands. "Look a'here, Sam," she said angrily, "I don't want to hear another word out of you. They've got to scrub the front porch and fix some bouquets and a lot else. A great big boy like you takin' on so over a little job like churnin'. Why, it's ridiculous."

Sammy Thax didn't answer. Sullenly he went on with his task. Surely the butter must be coming by now. He opened the lid and looked in. A skim of tiny particles of butter, no bigger than tomato seeds, was on top of the milk. Sammy Thax felt a little more hopeful. He fastened down the lid and churned faster. Just then he heard a long, low whistle. He looked up and saw Jud coming through the back gate with his fishing pole and his dog, Spot. Sammy Thax's ears burned. He didn't want Jud to see him with an apron on, churning. But there was nothing to do but face it, so he called, "C'mon in. I'll be through directly."

Jud finished swallowing a mouthful of gingerbread before he spoke. He handed a square of it, fresh and fragrant, to Sammy Thax and said, "Ma sent it to you. Hurry up and let's go."

Sammy Thax's mother had warned him not to open the churn, but he could not resist. "I think it's about come," he told Jud. He put down his gingerbread and opened the lid. Lumps of butter as big as butterbeans were floating on top. "Look a'there, Jud," he said. "All we need is a dipper of cold water to make it gather."

Jud rushed to the water bucket on a shelf by the kitchen door and brought back a brimming dipperful. He poured it into the churn. "Now turn it slow like," he said. "Ma goes slow to make it gather. Spot sure wants your gingerbread."

Sammy Thax turned and said, "Git away, Spot." He picked up the gingerbread and ate it hurriedly. Then he replaced the lid and gave the churn a twirl. Bang! The heavy lid flew off and hit Spot who gave a shrill yelp. Six gallons of buttermilk, with dabs of butter floating on top poured out and spread across the newly scrubbed back porch. Sammy Thax and Jud looked at each other like two badly scared rabbits. Jud said, "C'mon, Spot," and disappeared at once through the back gate.

Sammy Thax's mother rushed out of the kitchen, looking hot and tired and as mad as a wet hen. She grabbed Sammy Thax and shook him good

27

and hard. "Now, sir," she said to him, "you go straight to that woodpile and cut wood until I tell you to stop. No fishing for you today." She untied the apron strings and jerked the apron from around his neck and called, "Hester, Susan, come and clean up this mess. My stars in heaven." She looked ready to cry.

Sammy Thax did not loiter. He went to the woodpile and picked up the ax and set to work. He pulled a hickory sapling out of the uncut pile and dragged it to the chopping block. It was very hot. He wondered if Jud and Spot were on the way to the creek. It was cool down there, and Jud would bait his line and sit down under a big sycamore tree and listen to the creek make gurgling sounds like a happy baby and watch the water bugs skate over the surface and wait for the fish to bite. Chopping away, he thought about Robinson Crusoe. He wished he lived on an island, just he and Bowser, where there were no women to make slaves out of boys. The only one who didn't do that was Gran. He wouldn't mind having Gran on the island.

About that time he saw her going toward the hen house with one hand under her apron. The next he knew she came from behind the hen house and crooked her finger at him. He hurried over to her, and she handed him a piece of warm pound cake.

"Thank you, Gran," said Sammy Thax as he stuffed the cake in his mouth.

"I didn't mean to cut it till tomorrow," she said, "but it's no matter. I figured you need a bite now worse than the preacher needs to see a cake still uncut tomorrow."

Sammy Thax ate it quickly; it was delicious. Then he said, "Gran, I'm awful thirsty. Could you bring me a drink of water?"

"I'll fetch you some fresh from the pump," she said eagerly. She hurried off to the pump in the backyard. He heard the pump handle squeaking up and down. A minute later Gran came toward him with a gourd dipper brimming full. Sammy Thax gulped it down.

"Gran, I wisht you and me and Bowser lived on an island," he said.

Gran's eyes twinkled in her wrinkled face. "There's times I wouldn't mind it myself, to tell you the truth," she said. "But cheer up, Sammy, it ain't so long till dinner time now, and we've got a good peach cobbler for dessert."

Sammy Thax handed the empty dipper to her and looked at her uneasily. "Gran," he muttered accusingly. "Did you mail a letter to Aunt Minnie the day I went to the circus? Susan said you did. She said you are aimin' to go to Idaho and live with her." He lowered his head, ashamed that his lips were trembling.

"Poor Minnie needs me, Sammy, seein' she's a widow now with four younguns," Gran said. She fingered the edge of her apron and slid it rapidly back and forth between her thumb and forefinger as she always did when she was upset. "She says if I will come and take care of the children, she can teach the country school close by where she lives. The county superintendent named it to her."

"We need you too, Gran," blurted Sammy Thax. "I'd as lief be dead as live around here without you, Gran."

"Why, Sammy, the very idee," Gran said. "But it does make a body feel proud to know they would be missed. I ain't goin' right away though; that school don't start till about the end of August." Her lips were trembling too. She turned aside and hurried back to the kitchen.

Sammy Thax leaned on the ax handle and watched her go; then he walked back to the woodpile. He struck the sapling on the chopping block such a lick that a chip of it sailed ten feet. A tear rolled down his cheek. But his face brightened when he saw Rindy coming up from the woods below the barn. Rindy lived with his family in a small house near the creek. He was a good man, rather old and slow, but still a hard worker. His kind face broke into a smile when he saw Sammy Thax at the woodpile, and when he drew near he said, "Boy, they done got you workin' on a Sadday?" he asked. "Reckon can you stop long enough to turn the grindstone fur me a few minutes?"

Sammy Thax drove his ax blade into the chopping block and gladly followed Rindy to the toolshed close by. He knew his mother would not be mad if he stopped to help Rindy. The grindstone was a solid wheel of emery, mounted on a frame with a handle to turn it. Sammy Thax turned the stone slowly and steadily. Rindy held the edge of the big hoe against it, and the sparks flew. When the hoe was well sharpened, he set it aside and said, "Now lemme put an edge on your ax, and your choppin' will go faster. But mind you don't cut off any of your toes." He smiled and looked down at Sammy Thax's dusty, bare feet.

Silently, Sammy Thax turned the grinder while Rindy sharpened the ax. "Pears like you don't want to talk today, Sam," the old man said. "You look down in the mouth." He took from his pocket a plug of tobacco and cut off a small piece. As he fumbled with his knife, he dropped the little chew, and it disappeared into the high grass. He said, "Let it go, ain't worth huntin'," and cut off another piece.

"Give me a chew, Rindy," said Sammy Thax suddenly. The old man gave the boy a startled look. "What you talkin' about, boy?" he demanded. "You know your Pa don't believe in chewin' tobaccy."

"You are a real good man, Rindy, and you chew it," argued Sammy Thax sulkily. "When my Grandpa was alive, he told me that tobacco could sort of help a man forget his troubles."

Rindy's kind face wrinkled more as he smiled. He patted Sammy Thax on the back and chuckled. "He was stretchin' truth, boy," he said. "And you don't have no real troubles, not yet. All you need is finish your choppin' and take old Bowser and go fishin'. They is bound to be bitin' today." He shouldered his hoe and headed back toward the cornfield.

Sammy Thax watched him go, and his chin jutted out in a stubborn way. Grown people, except Gran, thought a boy didn't have any troubles. He kicked the grass at his feet and uncovered the piece of tobacco that Rindy had dropped. He picked it up, looked at it, glanced around to be sure he was alone, and popped it into his mouth. They could make him chop wood because he spilled the buttermilk. They could stop him from going fishing with Jud. But no one was going to stop him from chewing tobacco. In spite of himself, his nose wrinkled in disgust.

It didn't taste as nice as he thought it would. But he kept chewing away, and presently he spat a brown stream. He wanted to learn to spit as far as Rindy could.

Just then, like a bolt of lightning from a clear sky, his father rounded the corner of the toolshed. He said, "Well, Sam, you are a smart boy today. Glad to see you at it. It takes work to make a man."

Sammy Thax turned his head to one side, to hide the lump in his jaw, and his face grew very red. "What's that you're chewin'?" demanded his father, giving him a sharp look. Sammy Thax could think of only one thing to do, and he did it. With a gulp he swallowed the tobacco and answered "Nothin'."

"Worse than nothin,' appears to me," his father said. A terrible frown appeared on his face. Sammy Thax waited. Then, when all hope was lost, Hester came running from the orchard, calling to her father that the blind mule was tangled in the orchard fence. Mr. Milliken hurried off, and Sammy Thax sat down suddenly on the chopping block. He felt dizzy and sick at his stomach. He got sicker and sicker and sicker. He thought how bad his father was going to feel when he came back to give him a whipping and found him dead. When he stopped being sick, he stretched out on the ground and shut his eyes. The next he knew Gran was bending over him, speaking softly, "Sammy, air you sick? I didn't hear the ax goin', and I thought I'd best see about you. It's an awful hot mornin' for choppin' wood."

Sammy Thax told Gran the truth. He knew she wouldn't scold. She said, "Well, it's been a lesson to you, I reckon. Just lie there till you feel better." She looked up and saw Sammy Thax's father coming from the orchard, a peachtree switch in his hand. Her lips tightened, and she stood up stiff and straight and faced her son. "Now, Samuel Thaxton," she said to him, "Sammy done wrong, and he ain't likely to forget it soon. But, if I was you, I wouldn't punish him. Don't you mind the time, when you was his size, you took a notion to smoke your Pa's pipe? And he didn't lay a finger on you for it."

Mr. Milliken stood facing his mother with a frown. But finally a sheepish smile flitted over his face. He threw down the switch and walked toward the barn. "Just you lie still till you feel better Sammy," Gran said. "I doubt you'll want any dinner today. But I'll save you some peach cobbler for supper."

Pups for Sale
CHEAP

SAMMY THAX HAD TWO DOGS, BOWSER AND OLD
Fan. Old Fan was really old and nearly blind, but she
had five new puppies. Sammy Thax found them
when he went to the barn late one afternoon to col-
lect the eggs. They were lying on some hay in Old
Ned's stall. Sammy Thax thought they were the prettiest pups Old Fan had ever had. There were two
black and white ones and three that were solid black.
He wished he could keep them all, but when he told
his mother about them, she said, "Well, you better
start lookin' for homes for them. We don't need another dog. Two dogs is enough. More than enough."

Every morning Sammy Thax went to the barn

to see the pups. He decided that the prettiest one was the one with a white spot on his forehead, white feet, and a white tip on his tail. But all of them were pretty and healthy, and he decided to try to sell them for fifty cents each. The next morning Susan overheard him telling Gran that he was going to sell the pups. She laughed and said, "You'll be lucky if you can give them away. Who do you think would buy a puppy?"

"Plenty of people," said Sammy Thax hotly. "A lot you know about pups, Susan Milliken." Giving her a scornful look, Sammy Thax went to the toolshed to make a sign. He found a piece of pine plank, sawed it off, and with a stiff and stubby little paintbrush and some of the black paint left over from painting the surrey, he lettered a sign: "PUPS FOR SALE CHEAP." He took the sign, still wet, and nailed it to the gatepost, near the mailbox. On the way back to the house he thought about what he would do with the money. He would buy Gran a black silk umbrella to take to Idaho. Her old one was split to pieces.

But it wasn't just the money that Sammy Thax had in mind. He was afraid that if he didn't get rid of the pups by the time they were weaned, they would be put to death. Other times when Old Fan had a litter if nobody wanted them, they just disappeared.

He suspected that Rindy drowned them in the creek on his father's orders, but Rindy wouldn't confess. He would just shake his head and say, "Beats me where they went to, Sam."

He decided he would hold back on selling his favorite pup until the other four were sold. Maybe then he could persuade his mother to let him keep that one. He had named him Domino because of his white dots. Since Old Fan might die any time and Bowser was a middle-aged dog, they really needed a pup. It seemed to him his mother would see that.

The day after he put up his sign, he had to go to mill and take a sack of shelled corn to be ground into cornmeal. Before he left, he got Gran to go with him to the barn. He showed her the litter. She agreed that Domino was the prettiest and should be kept. He said to her, "If anybody comes to buy a pup while I'm gone, don't sell him. You take the money and keep it for me and tell them I'll deliver the pups when they are six weeks old."

"I'll do the best I can for you, Sammy," said Gran. "But don't get out of heart if you don't sell any right off. It might take a little time."

There were several ahead of him at the mill, so it was the middle of the afternoon before he got home with his sack of meal. Gran met him at the kitchen door. She led the way to the pantry and gave him some freshly baked teacakes. "Did you sell any?" asked Sammy Thax, wolfing down the cookies.

"Not for cash money," Gran said, "but the little Hoffstetter boy came by, Franz—that's his name. He said they have a runt bull calf born yesterday, and Mr. Hoffstetter wants to be rid of it. With all those cows in their dairy they have too many calves. He said he will trade you the new calf for a pup."

"Domino?" asked Sammy Thax anxiously.

"I told him that one wasn't for sale or trade," said Gran, twinkling. "So he picked one of the solid black ones. I tied a red string around his neck to mark him."

"Will Pa let me have the calf?" asked Sammy Thax. "What will I raise him on?"

"You talk to your Pa," said Gran. "Bossy's calf is ready to be weaned, so maybe she could suckle him. She's a good mother, and she would take him."

After supper that night Sammy Thax talked it over with his father, and Mr. Milliken agreed to let him have the calf. Very early the next morning Sammy Thax and Jud walked two miles to the Hoffstetter's big farm, the biggest and best farm in the neighborhood. Franz saw them coming and ran to meet them. "You want'er trade, huh?" he asked.

Sammy Thax nodded. "But the pups are too young yet."

"I know," nodded Franz. "I'll come and get mine in about four weeks. But you have to take the calf today. I'll help you get him home."

Sammy Thax and Jud followed Franz to the barn. Mr. Hoffstetter was there, a big man with a booming voice. "Vell," he said, "here's the livestock traders. Now this calf, he's sort of a runt, but you take him and vork on him, Sam, and he might get you a blue ribbon at the fair." He opened a stall door, and there was the calf. He looked so weak and wobbly that Sammy Thax was taken aback. But he had never had a calf of his own before, and he felt proud to know that this one was his. "Can I drive him home?" he asked Mr. Hoffstetter.

"No, no, he ain't dat strong yet," said Mr. Hoffstetter. "You and him and Jud can ride back wid me on der vagon. I'm going to town soon."

The boys put some hay in the back of the wagon and lifted the calf onto it. Then they sat, one on each side of him, stroking him and talking over the trade with Franz. "My cousin Phil, well he wants a pup if he can get one free," said Franz.

Jud said, "Give him that spotted female, Sam. You can't sell her."

"You tell him he can have her, Franz," said Sammy Thax. "Ma is gettin' fussy about the pups. She don't like dogs. Ain't that queer?"

Franz nodded. "Women, well they are afraid of tracks on the floor," he agreed. "My mother says I've got to keep my pup outdoors. I'm building me a doghouse."

Mr. Hoffstetter said it was time to go. Franz climbed up beside his father for the trip to town. Sammy Thax and Jud rode in the wagon bed with the calf. When they got home and unloaded the calf, Sammy Thax's father looked at him and shook his head. "Well, Sam," he said, "since you just traded a pup for him, he'll do. But he is a weakly little fellow if ever I saw one. What are you going to name him?"

"Samson," answered Sammy Thax. "That's for that strong man in the Bible that Gran reads me about. I mean to make him get big and strong."

"Samson," said Mr. Milliken with a smile, "hmm, well, that's a good name. You might say it means Sam's son, and I guess you mean to be a father to him."

Jud helped Sammy Thax get the calf into a clean stall, and the two boys, with Mr. Milliken's permission, drove Bossy in from the pasture and into the stall with the calf. In spite of her name, she was a gentle old cow. She nuzzled the baby calf as if he had been her own. The boys held him up and let him suck. "That's enough milk for him, I reckon, till suppertime. I'll put her back in here with him tonight." They turned Bossy out, and she ambled off to the pasture.

"Let's see the pups," suggested Jud. "I wish I could have one. But Ma would make me bring it right back." He sighed. "This is the one I want." He reached over and picked up Domino.

"He's mine," said Sammy Thax quickly. "He ain't for sale."

"I thought your Ma said get rid of all of them," said Jud.

"She did," admitted Sammy Thax. "But I'm still hopin' she will change."

"She won't," grumbled Jud. "She's just like my Ma."

In the week that followed, no one came to buy a pup. Late one afternoon Sammy Thax was at the barn attending to Samson when Rindy came along. "I can't sell these pups, Rindy," said Sammy Thax. "I wisht you would help me give them away."

"My little grandson that lives with us, he wants a dog," said Rindy. "And seems to me like my wife said the widow woman across the creek is needin' a watchdog."

"Old Fan is a good watchdog," said Sammy Thax. "She don't bite, but she makes people think she will. I bet these pups will be like her."

So the next day Rindy took two pups home with him, and that left only Domino. Sammy Thax thought he was the cutest pup he had ever seen. And Old Fan might not ever have another litter. She seemed to get thinner and weaker every day. They needed a pup to remember Fan by. Sammy told his mother, but she only shook her head.

School would start the first week in August. Miss Effie Andrews was the teacher, a tall, slender woman with a voice that could crack like a whip when her pupils misbehaved. One afternoon she came to the Millikens'. Sammy Thax met her at the door, invited her in, and took her into the parlor. When his mother came in, Sammy Thax started to leave, but Miss Andrews said firmly, "Sit down, Sammy Thax. I came to see you, as well as your mother." Sammy Thax sat down, feeling uneasy. His teacher explained that she wanted to have a speaking contest and a box supper at the school the first Friday night in August, to raise money for window shades in the schoolroom. She handed Mrs. Milliken a copy of a poem, "The Midnight Ride of Paul Revere." She glanced at Sammy Thax and smiled. "That's what I want Samuel Thaxton to recite in the contest," she said. "It is a piece most everyone likes to hear spoken."

Sammy Thax looked at his mother and frowned, but she paid no attention to him. "He will be glad to," Mrs. Milliken said. "I'll set him to work on it right away."

Miss Effie got up to leave. Mrs. Milliken invited her to stay to supper, but she said she must go on to Watsons'. They were expecting her.

When she had gone, Sammy Thax turned to his mother with a scowl. "Why did you tell her I would say a speech?" he growled.

"Why, Sam, for shame," cried his mother. "It's an honor to be asked to speak a piece in the contest. You might win the prize. Wouldn't Gran be proud?"

"Jesse Watson will get the prize," said Sammy Thax sourly. "He likes to say speeches." His mother stood looking at his sulky face and raised a finger to her lips. "I tell you what," she said, "if you will learn that poem by heart and do your best in the contest, I'll let you keep the spotted pup."

Sammy Thax's face lighted up. "Cross your heart and hope to die?" he demanded.

"I cross my heart and hope to die I'll keep my word," his mother said. She handed him the poem. "Here it is; don't misplace it. Learn it by heart and practice it every day."

Sammy Thax, poem in hand, went upstairs to his grandmother's room. She was there, mending one of his shirts. He drew up the footstool and sat down beside her. "Gran, guess what?" he said. "If I learn

43

this poem by heart and speak it at school, Ma says I can keep Domino. Will you help me learn it?"

"Of course I will, Sammy," she answered, looking at him over the top of her spectacles. "I'll be proud to help you."

That evening and every evening after supper Sammy Thax and his grandmother worked on the poem. It didn't take him long to memorize it, and he practiced it over and over until Gran knew it too. One night she said, "Now I want you to say it for the family. I want them to hear you."

Sammy Thax hung his head. "I don't want to," he said.

"Think about Domino," she urged. "If you practice before the family, you won't be afraid of the crowd that night."

So the next night, right after supper, Gran asked everybody to be quiet and listen to Sammy recite the poem. His face was red, and he spoke very fast in a low voice.

"Don't mumble," cried Hester.

"Speak louder, son," said Pa.

"Go slow," said Susan.

"Raise your head," said Ma.

Only Gran was silent. Her lips moved as she followed the words with him, and she wrung her hands because she couldn't help him. The next morning after breakfast his father said, "Come with me, Sam. I want to talk to you." He led the way to the barn. Sammy Thax held his breath. He thought his father might tell him that Domino was gone, or Samson was dead. Instead Mr. Milliken turned around and smiled at him and said, "I wanted to be out of hearing of the women folks. I want to help you with your speech. Gran don't know much about elocution, but I won a medal once for public speaking. And I know that poem of yours by heart." He stood on a wooden box by the feed room door. He cleared his throat and drew a deep breath. His voice rolled out, big and strong, *"Listen, my children, and you shall hear of the midnight ride of Paul Revere."* Sammy Thax stared at his father in surprise, and Mr. Milliken, without faltering, recited the whole poem. When he finished, he said, "Now Sam, you try it. Get up there in the feed trough and let me hear you."

In a singsong voice Sammy Thax began, *"Listen my children, and you shall hear."* "Louder, Sam," said his father. *"Of the midnight ride of Paul Revere,"* shouted Sammy Thax.

"That's better," said his father. "Go ahead."

Daily, Mr. Milliken made Sammy Thax rehearse with only himself and Domino and Samson for an audience. On the last morning he said, "Don't get rattled, and you'll do fine. May win the prize."

When the day of the contest came, Hester and Susan worked all day preparing box suppers for that night. Sammy Thax's mother pressed his Sunday suit, shined his shoes, and cut his hair. Gran got out her black silk dress and her bonnet with jet beads on it. When night came, they all squeezed into the surrey and drove to the Greenglade schoolhouse. A big crowd was gathering, and soon the schoolhouse was packed. The stage was decorated with wilting flowers and a United States flag.

The seven boys who were to speak in the contest sat on the platform in a semicircle of chairs. Sammy Thax was scared. His mouth felt dry. His heart pounded against his ribs like a captured bird. He stared at the floor and put one foot on top of the other.

Jesse Watson spoke first. The name of his piece was "Excelsior." He was not afraid. He threw back his head and rolled his eyes, and his voice filled the big room. When he finished, the crowd clapped, and Jesse bowed like the man who was running for governor had at a speaking. Sammy Thax hated Jesse. The next boy was John Baxter. He recited "The Boy Stood on the Burning Deck." He knew how to make it sound pitiful, though he was not as good a speaker as Jesse.

Then it was Sammy Thax's turn. He was as

white as a sheet. His shoes creaked as he walked to his place. On the front row sat his father and mother and Gran. Sammy Thax stood there, licking his lips. Domino or no Domino, the words would not come. He had forgotten them. He saw Gran's lips moving. His mother's eyes were closed. His father leaned forward and said in a low tone, "Listen, my children, and you shall hear." Sammy Thax gulped. He did not raise his head or lift his eyes. He muttered, "Listen, my children, and you shall hear." Everyone listened. You could have heard a pin fall. But nobody heard anything more from Sammy Thax. Slowly he turned around and went creaking back to his seat and sat down. He stole a look at Gran. She was dabbing at her eyes with a handkerchief.

On the way home no one spoke of the contest or the box supper. Hester and Susan were quiet. Sammy Thax sat hunched down between them and did not say a word. When they got home, he went straight upstairs to his room, took off his Sunday clothes, and went to bed. After a while Gran came softly in and patted his shoulders and said, "Never mind, Sammy."

The next morning before breakfast Sammy Thax went to the barn to see about Samson. The little calf was doing well. Bossy loved him. Then he went to the stall where Old Fan lay. He picked up Domino. The puppy licked his face. His father looked in: he had a full pail of foaming fresh milk in his hand. "You here, Sam?" he asked. "I allowed you were still asleep."

"Johnny Baxter wants this pup," said Sammy Thax. "If I've got to get rid of him, I'll give him to Johnny."

Mr. Milliken set his bucket of milk on a shelf by the door. He came over and laid a hand on Sammy Thax's head. "Your Ma and I talked it over last night," he said. "We decided to let you keep him. In a way you earned him." When he had gone, Sammy Thax hugged the fat wriggling pup so hard that he gave a yelp.

Sad Day
in August

USUALLY ON A BRIGHT SUMMER MORNING SAMMY Thax was up with the birds. He loved to go outside in the cool early light, just before sunup, and run barefooted through the wet grass with Bowser at his heels. He loved to go to the orchard and eat some fruit, if only green apples. But that morning, when he waked at dawn, he lay still, frowning and dreading something. What was it? He blinked his eyes, and as he came fully awake, he remembered and groaned. This was the day Gran was leaving for Idaho. He rolled over and buried his head in his pillow. He didn't want to get up. He lay there until Hester put her head in the door and called, "You'd better get up, Sam, if you aim to go to the depot with us. Breakfast is about ready."

Sammy Thax got up. Then he sat back down on the side of his bed and stared out the window. Ever since he was born, Gran had lived with them. Even when Grandpa was alive, they both lived there. Every night it was Gran who heard him say his prayers and tucked him in bed. Gran never got cross at him; she always understood things. And when he came in hungry from school, Gran always had a piece of pie or some teacakes for him. When he accidently tore his pants, Gran mended them so you could hardly see the place. Her room was just across the hall from his. Often at night when she was in there knitting or mending or reading her Bible, he would go and sit near on the footstool. Sometimes she would tell him tales of the times when she was young, tales about big campmeetings and log rollings and quilting bees and spelling matches. She would tell him about the shooting matches and bear hunts and about the wild turkeys that used to be plentiful and pigeons in great flocks that would darken the sky as they flew over. Sometimes she would tell him tales about the Civil War, and tears would come to her eyes. In her squeaky, old voice she would sing, "The Bonny Blue Flag." There were other songs she would sing that Sammy

Thax loved—"Seeing Nellie Home," "My Bonnie Lies over the Ocean," "Flow Gently, Sweet Afton."

Every night during the school term she helped him with his lessons. Especially she drilled him on spelling. "It's a sign you are educated, if you can spell proper, Sammy," she would tell him. Often as he and Jud walked to school together, Sammy Thax would brag to Jud, "My Gran is real smart. She knows about geography and history and spelling, and she knows the multiplication tables backward and forward."

He put his head in his hands. His mother's voice, loud and a little cross, called up the stairs, "Sam-*mee!* If you don't come on down to breakfast right now, you won't get a bite." Sammy Thax, for once, didn't want a bite. He had a lump in his throat as big as a hen egg and a sick, hollow feeling at the pit of his stomach. But he dressed and went down to the dining room.

Everyone else in the family was already half through breakfast. Sammy Thax stole a look at Gran. Instead of her usual clean gray and white calico dress, she had on her black silk with a white lace collar pinned together with a round breastpin that had a picture of Grandpa in it. She was sipping her coffee and rolling a crumb of biscuit in her fingers. She wasn't eating any breakfast. Sammy Thax thought Gran must have a lump in *her* throat as big as his. Everyone else was eating and talking as usual. Sammy Thax didn't see how they could, when Gran was leaving.

"If you think you are going to the depot with us in your overalls you are mistaken," Hester said. "Go put on your Sunday clothes. And hurry."

"That's right, hurry, Sam," his mother said. "It's nearly time to go."

Sammy Thax went up to his room. He didn't want to go to the depot. He didn't want to see Gran get on the train to go to Idaho. He might not ever see her again. He lay down on the bed and pulled the pillow over his head. Presently he felt a hand on his shoulder. He lifted the pillow. Gran was standing beside the bed, looking down at him. "Ain't you goin' with us, Sammy?" she asked. He shook his head. "Now, Sammy, I was countin' on you goin'," Gran said. "And after the train leaves and all, you go by Mehaffey's soda fountain and buy some soda pop and some peppermint sticks." She slipped three nickels into his hand and went to her room.

Sammy Thax got up and dressed in his best clothes. He slicked his hair down with water, the way Gran liked it, and went to her room. She took a quick look at him and said, "My, you look nice. I wish I had a picture of you to take to Idyho with me." She put on her Sunday bonnet and tied the ribbons under her chin. "You want to take my satchel for me?" she asked. "Your Pa and Rindy took my trunk down and tied it on the back of the surrey real early this mornin.' I hope they got it on there good and stout."

Downstairs, Hester and Susan were waiting, dressed up and twittering with excitement. Sammy Thax thought they were the silliest girls he had ever seen. His father was dressed in his best, and he escorted Gran down the front steps and out the brick walk to the gate where Rindy was waiting with the team and surrey. He had washed the surrey in Gran's honor and oiled the harness and hitched up Old Ned and the younger horse, Chigger.

Gran shook hands with Rindy and thanked him for what he had done. He bowed and said, "Ma'am, we is all goin' to miss you, that's certain." He and Mr. Milliken helped her up into the front seat, and Mr. Milliken sat down beside her. Hester and Susan and Sammy Thax took the back seat. Sammy Thax's mother was not going with them. She said she had to stay at home and churn and gather the vegetables before it got too hot. But she followed Gran to the gate and after she was in the surrey, handed her a big shoe box, neatly tied with a ribbon. "Gran, here's enough food, I hope, to last you till you get there," she said. "Write to us." Sammy Thax saw his mother hastily wipe her eyes on her apron. Gran thanked her and said she would write. Rindy lifted his old straw hat and waved his free hand in farewell as they drove off. Rindy had very good manners.

His father said little. All the way to town Gran was silent and so was Sammy Thax, but Hester and Susan chattered away. The early August morning was bright and cloudless; the fences along the road were hung with devil's shoestring and its long red flowers like trumpets. Black-eyed susans grew beside the road, along with Queen Anne's lace. But Sammy Thax's eyes were dull. He did not pay attention to anything on that ride. He felt worse than he had on the day of the circus when he found that his money was gone. He swallowed hard when they came in sight of the Richfield depot, a little yellow building close to the tracks.

Mr. Milliken drew the horses to a stop and said, "You hitch them, Sam, while I get the trunk unloaded." Mr. Milliken helped his mother to the ground and escorted her into the station. Hester and Susan sprang from the surrey and shook out their full skirts and starched petticoats. A friendly bystander helped Mr. Milliken get the trunk to the baggage platform. Sammy Thax hitched the team and went into the waiting room. He sat down and stared at a fly-specked picture of Niagara Falls. Gran was at the ticket window. Presently she came and sat by Sammy Thax. The girls moved and sat on the other side of her. They talked to Gran, but Sammy Thax had nothing to say. Not even when Mrs. Pringle, the preacher's wife, strolled into the station to say good-bye to Gran.

When he heard the train whistle, a shiver went through him. Everyone stood up, looking nervous. They all went outside and watched the train approaching. Sammy Thax thought he knew why it was called the iron horse. When it stopped, it seemed to be panting. He bit on his forefinger to hide his trembling lips. Gran gave Hester and Susan and their father each a quick kiss. Last of all she kissed Sammy Thax and whispered, "You be a good boy, Sammy. Write me a letter." He nodded and muttered, "Goodbye, Gran."

"All aboard," called the conductor, watch in hand. There was no one to go aboard but Gran. The conductor helped her up the steep steps, and she disappeared into the day coach. She got a seat near a window and timidly waved her hand as the train, with a loud hissing of steam and flying sparks, began to move. They all stood still until it rounded a curve and passed out of sight.

Sammy Thax went to the surrey and climbed

into the front seat. He wanted to go home. He didn't want any soda pop or candy. He meant to get Bowser and go down to the creek where nobody could see him cry. Even Hester and Susan cried a little and were almost quiet on the way home. Mr. Milliken blew his nose and cleared his throat and didn't talk at all.

When they got home, Sammy Thax hurried upstairs and changed into his overalls. He hung his Sunday clothes carefully, as Gran had taught him to do. The door of her room was open. The narrow bed was neatly made, and her rocking chair, with its faded red cushion, stood near the window. Sammy Thax quickly closed the door. He didn't intend to go into that room again until Gran came home, if she ever did.

Something for Gran

THE NEXT MORNING SAMMY THAX ATE ONLY A few bites of breakfast, and he got out of the house as quickly as he could. Gran's gray chambray sunbonnet was hanging on its peg on the back porch, and when he saw it, Sammy Thax hurried by as if he had seen a ghost. He was standing in the backyard when his mother came in from the garden. She took a quick look at his miserable face and said briskly, "Sam, why don't you go over and see Jud this morning? I don't know as I need you around here."

It was a rare day when his mother didn't have a job for him, so Sammy Thax whistled for Bowser, and the two of them set off across the fields for

Jud's house. They found Jud's mother sitting on her cool back porch, peeling sugar pears for preserves. "Come in, Sam," she said. She handed him a pear. "Jud's down in the cellar, fetching me some fruit jars." "He'll be up in a few minutes. Well, I guess your grandma got off to Idaho yesterday?" Sammy Thax nodded. "I hope she's satisfied way off up there with Minnie and those children," she said, "but I doubt it. It ain't so easy for old people to leave their birthplace and their lifelong friends. I don't doubt she'll be mighty homesick."

Sammy Thax squirmed. He didn't want to talk about Gran. He didn't want to think how that train was right now taking her farther and farther from home. The day before, when she was leaving, it sounded as if the train wheels were saying over and over, "To Idaho, to Idaho, to Idaho." He was glad when Jud came up from the cellar with a basket of empty, dusty jars in his hand. Jud's face brightened when he saw Sammy Thax.

"Hey, c'mon, Sammy," he said. "I'll show you where I found the guinea hen's nest. It had fourteen eggs in it. Ma's goin' to let 'em alone and let the hen set on 'em and hatch 'em out."

"Take these pear peelin's and feed them to the pig," his mother said. "And, Sammy Thax, you stay and eat dinner with us. You boys listen for the dinner bell and come straight to the house. Don't get out of hearin'."

School would start on Monday, and the two boys dreaded it. They hated for the summer vacation to end. They decided to go fishing the next day, which was Saturday.

After the big noon dinner, Sammy Thax went home. When he got there, he saw a strange horse and buggy at the gate, and a strange man coming up the walk. He went to meet him, and the man said politely, "Good afternoon. Is the lady of the house at home?"

"Yessir," said Sammy Thax, leading the way to the front door. The man followed him into the parlor and took a chair. Sammy Thax went to get his mother who was busy in the kitchen. He wondered where Hester and Susan were. "Ma," he said, "It's a man in the parlor, and he wants to see you." Hurriedly, Mrs. Milliken washed her hands and smoothed her hair. She took off her checked apron and followed Sammy Thax to the parlor.

The man sprang to his feet and bowed politely. He said, "Ma'am, my name is Henry Henderson, and I am a photographer. I'd like to show you some pictures I have made, if you have a little time to spare."

"Well, I don't mind if you do," said Mrs.

Milliken. So, before you could say scat, the man opened a little flat suitcase he had with him and took out some photographs. The first one was a picture of a bride in a white dress, with a veil. She wore a locket and chain, and they were gilded. She held a bouquet of roses.

"I wish my daughters were here; I might have a picture of them made," said Mrs. Milliken. "My, you do pretty work."

"Will they be back soon?" asked the man. Mrs. Milliken shook her head. "They've gone over to my sister's place, near Ferndale, to spend the night. She's got a daughter about their age."

Quickly, the man selected another picture and handed it to her. It was of a boy about Sammy Thax's age, dressed in a sailor suit. He was standing beside a table which had a toy ship with flags on it. Sammy Thax leaned on his mother's shoulder and looked at it with her. "What about your son, here?" asked the man. "I bet you don't have a picture of him, now do you?"

"Just his baby picture," said Mrs. Milliken.

"A handsome boy like that and you don't have a picture of him?" cried the man as if he was shocked. "You'd better let me make his picture today, Madam. I won't be back this way anytime soon."

When they started talking about the price and

dickering a little, Sammy Thax eased out the door and started toward the barn. He didn't want to have his picture taken. But before he got out of hearing, his mother called, "Come back here, Sam. Where are you going?" He turned around and came back, dragging his feet. "We are going to have your picture taken," his mother said nervously. "Come along, I'll help you get dressed up."

"Aw, Ma," whined Sammy Thax, embarrassed, "I don't want my pitcher taken."

"It's a chance that don't come every day, Sam," his mother said, pushing him along to the stairs. "I mean to have it framed and hang it in the parlor." Upstairs she made him wash, then she hustled him into his wintertime Sunday suit and the shirt with a ruffle down the front that Gran had made him. She made him put on his Sunday shoes, which had gotten to be too tight, and she brushed his hair the way she liked it.

As he followed his mother back downstairs, Sammy Thax felt like a dunce. He had never been called handsome by anyone but this man. He had freckles all over his face, and his ears were too big and stuck out from his head. The man had just said that Sammy was handsome to please his mother. He only wanted to make some money. Sammy Thax eyed the photographer in an unfriendly way as he hurried around setting up his camera on a tall stand and covering it with a black cloth. He spread a wrinkled piece of flowered velvet over a parlor chair and asked Sammy Thax to sit down. He got behind his camera and put his head under the black cloth. Sammy Thax sat like a statue. The man jumped out and rearranged his hands and feet and told him to smile. A fixed and foolish grin was all Sammy Thax could manage. He had about as soon have a tooth pulled. Finally the man jumped out again, rubbing his hands and saying, "Splendid. Now, let's take a standing position."

Mrs. Milliken stood by, beaming. The man had Sammy Thax stand by the parlor center table, on which stood the tall brass lamp with a pink glass shade. He tilted Sammy's head to one side and told him to look right at the camera. Finally, he said, "There you are. You are going to be pleased, Ma'am, when you see these proofs. I feel sure you will want one of each. The second one is cheaper of course." He figured on a piece of paper and handed it to her. Sammy Thax scowled. He didn't like Mr. Henry Henderson at all.

He was glad to see him load up his camera and drive off down the road toward Jud's. He grinned as he wondered if Jud would have to have his picture taken next. He hustled upstairs and got out of his

Sunday clothes and tight shoes and put on his hickory shirt and overalls. He went downstairs and out the back door and whistled for Bowser. A rabbit sprang out of the raspberry briers, and Domino gave a joyful yip and started after him.

Suddenly Sammy Thax remembered something. He turned around and ran back to the house. His mother was still in the parlor, holding in her hands the paper on which the man had figured the prices. "If your picture turns out real good, I'll have it enlarged and hang it over the mantel," she said.

"I don't want you to," said Sammy Thax, out of breath.

"Well, what *do* you want?" asked his mother impatiently.

"I want you to send it to Gran in Idaho, for Christmas," Sammy Thax said. "Gran told me she wished she had a picture of me to take."

"Well, I'm not sendin' any great big framed picture to Idaho," his mother said. "It costs too much, and like as not, Minnie's children would be careless and break the glass. I'm goin' to hang it in this parlor where it rightly belongs."

Sammy Thax stood silent, looking angrily at his mother. "Gran wants one," he repeated. "Gran don't never get a present." He swallowed hard. His mother's face softened. She said, looking at the piece of paper, "The man wants to make an extry one, smaller, to go in the family album. I'll let him do that, and we'll send it to your Gran for Christmas. We'll send album and all. It's rightly hers anyway."

Sammy Thax nodded. He knew that Gran, way up in Idaho, would love to have the family album. He was glad his picture would be in it. He knew it would be Gran's favorite picture.

Mail
from Idaho

IT WAS SEPTEMBER. GOLDEN ROD WAS IN BLOOM. and along the fence rows sasafras leaves were turning red. Gran had been gone a month. The family had had one letter from her when she first got to Idaho, to let them know she had arrived safely, but not another word.

Sammy Thax missed her more and more. When he came in from school, no one met him at the back door, as Gran had always done. No one had teacakes ready in the pantry. At night when it was time to study his lessons, he missed her. No one else seemed to have time to help him with his arithmetic problems or hear his spelling lesson.

One day, Miss Effie kept him in after school. She gave him a lecture: "Samuel Thaxton, you used to be near the head of the class in spelling. Now you are at the foot. Why? You used to draw neat, pretty maps in geography and now you don't. Why? You used to have your arithmetic problems worked out correctly; now you miss the answers half the time. What in the world has got into you?"

Sammy Thax hung his head. "I dunno, Miss Effie," he mumbled. He wouldn't tell her that it was because Gran was gone. "Well, if you don't try harder, you are going to fail your grade this year," she said. "And what would your folks say to that?" Sammy Thax didn't answer. "You know what your mother would say," Miss Effie told him; "she would say you were a lazy boy, and I've decided you are a lazy boy. Now here is a list of your spelling words for tomorrow. Write each word ten times for me. That will help you remember how to spell them. Sit down. Here is paper and pencil. I'll work on grading some papers."

Sammy Thax wet his pencil in his mouth and went to work. He glanced at Miss Effie. He thought she looked like a turkey hen. He thought she was a very hardhearted woman.

That night after supper Sammy went up to his room and got out his tablet and pencil to write a letter to Gran. He would not tell her he had been kept in after school. That would worry her. He had never written a letter to anyone before. He chewed on his pencil a while, and then he wrote:

> *Dear Gran.*
> *How are you? I sure miss you. School is hard. Samson is growing. Pa says he is going to make a good bull. Old Fan died. We berried her in the orchard. Domino is smart. He can shake hands. When are you coming home?*
>
> > *Your grandson Sammy T. Milliken*

He folded his letter, and then he remembered the four-leaf clover he had found in the orchard and put in his geography to press. He took it out and put it carefully inside his letter. The next morning after breakfast he asked his mother for an envelope. She said, "What for?"

"I wrote a letter to Gran," he answered.

"Give it to me," his mother said. "I think Susan has got some envelopes. I'll back it for you. I've been laying off addressing a letter to Gran myself."

Sammy Thax waited until his mother got an envelope and addressed it. She gave him some pennies for a stamp. He took the letter and set out for the post office. The post office was in a corner of Mr. Lem Thompson's country store, a mile beyond the schoolhouse. Mr. Lem was a short, fat, friendly man. He was sitting on the porch of his store when Sammy Thax got there that morning. He said, "Well, Sam, you're my first customer today."

Sammy Thax handed him the letter and the pennies. Mr. Lem read the name and address. "Your grandma is goin' to be proud to get this, I expect," he said. "I'm sure she is homesick, 'way off up there." He got up and waddled inside, stamped the letter, and put it in a box. "The mail carrier will be along tomorrow," he told Sammy Thax. He handed him a peppermint stick. "Here's a stick of candy to munch on your way to school."

"Thank you, Mr. Lem," said Sammy Thax. "You won't forget my letter, will you?"

"No sirree," said Mr. Lem, returning to his chair on the sunny porch. "If there's one thing I'm particular about, it's the U.S. mail."

Sammy Thax waited impatiently to get an answer to his letter. The mail was brought out from town to the store only twice a week, on Monday and Thursday. So each Monday and Thursday Sammy Thax went to the store after school to ask for the mail. One Monday the Sears Roebuck catalog came. Every Thursday the county paper came. But except for one letter to Susan from her beau, there were no letters. Three weeks went by. Then one afternoon when Sammy entered the store, Mr. Lem said, "I've got a letter here for Samuel Thaxton Milliken, Junior. Do you know him?"

Sammy Thax grinned as Mr. Milliken reached into one of the pigeon holes over his desk and drew out a letter. Sammy Thax's heart hammered when he saw Gran's handwriting on the envelope. He took his letter and hurried out. He went down the road to the big fallen sycamore tree, sat down, and carefully pried open the envelope. It was the first letter he ever received. He read:

> *Dear Sammy.*
>
> *Your welcome letter came to hand. Was glad to hear from you. Was sorry to hear Old Fan had died, but she had a long life. Glad you have got one of her pups. Idaho is a lot different from Tennessee. No close neighbors here. It is cold as winter time now. We had a deep snow last night. I don't like to see snow start so early. I dread the long winter. Minnie is teaching. The little girls, Sally and Jane, go with her in the buggy. The little boy, Johnny, and the baby stays with me all day. I bake teacakes like I made you with nutmeg on top. I stay busy.*
>
> *Be a good boy, Sammy. Study hard. Love to all,*
>
> *Gran*

MAIL
LETTERS
HERE

Sammy Thax returned the letter to its envelope and put it inside his geography. When he got home, he found his mother in the kitchen making green tomato pickle. The kitchen smelled good and spicy.

"I got a letter from Gran," Sammy Thax said, opening his geography and taking it out.

"You *did!*" his mother exclaimed. "Well, I want to read it. How is Gran?" Sammy Thax handed her the letter, and she sat down in a kitchen chair and adjusted her spectacles. "Gran writes a good hand for her age," she said. She read the letter aloud. "Gran sounds homesick to me," she said. "She's too old to be takin' care of real young children. And too old to stand hard winters. But then, go she would, to help Minnie."

"Ma, do you miss Gran?" asked Sammy Thax shyly.

"Miss Gran? Of course, I do!" said his mother. "She was a sight of help and company to me. And Gran never meddled nor complained like some old folks do."

"Will she ever come home?" asked Sammy Thax.

"Well, I can't answer that," his mother said. She got up and went to the stove to stir the pickle. "I don't see how Minnie can teach school without somebody to care for the children, and she's obliged to earn a livin' for them. Her husband was a poor man. When the children get older, Gran might come home, if she lives that long."

Those words, "if she lives that long," hit Sammy Thax with a stinging thud. He took his letter and went up to his room. He lay down across his bed and stared out the window. He wished he could run away to Idaho. He could shovel the snow for Gran and get in wood and kindling and water from the well. But he knew if he did that, his father would come and get him and bring him home, and he would never hear the last of it. He remembered what Gran used to say to him sometimes, "If wishes were horses, beggars would ride."

His mother called from the foot of the stairs, "Sam, come on now and get in the stove wood. It's fixin' to rain." Sammy Thax got up and went to the oak washstand. He opened the drawer and took out a tin box in which he kept his treasures—a pretty agate marble, his wallet, and an Indian arrowhead he had found near Rindy's house. Gently he laid Gran's letter in the tin box and turned the key.

The Beatin'est Cow

ONE SUNDAY NIGHT IN OCTOBER, MR. ALEC Apple's cow, Sudie, jumped the fence and got into the lower cornfield on the Milliken farm. That was very bad because the corn and pumpkins had not been gathered, and Sudie helped herself. Just about daylight Monday morning, Rindy discovered her and tried to get her out, but he failed. He came and called Mr. Milliken and told him the trouble.

Mr. Milliken said, "That cow will be the ruin of me yet." He rushed upstairs and found Sammy Thax sitting on the side of the bed, barely awake. "Jump up, son, get your clothes on quick," he said. "Sudie is in the lower cornfield again. I wish she would eat so much corn she'd founder. She is the peskiest cow that ever lived."

Sleepy and dazed, Sammy Thax pulled on his clothes and followed his father downstairs to where Rindy was waiting. His mother was cooking breakfast. Only Hester and Susan were still asleep. Girls, thought Sammy Thax frowning, always get to do just as they please.

Bowser, pleased to see them up and stirring, sprang up and followed the men and Sammy Thax to the cornfield. As they all approached her, the cow snorted and lunged off toward the far end of the field, tramping cornstalks and pumpkins as she went. Bowser ran after her, nipping at her heels and barking ferociously.

"Drat her hide," yelled Mr. Milliken. "Head her off, Sam; head her back this way. You can outrun me and Rindy. And make that dog shut up. Make him go back to the house. He makes everything worse." He leaned against a fence post to catch his breath.

"Hush your mouth, Bowser," panted Sammy Thax, as he stumbled through the cornfield. "Go home, dog." He called softly to the cow: "Sook cow, sook, sook." Bowser rolled his eyes and slunk away, but the cow went merrily on, tossing her head impudently as she ran past Sammy Thax. There was a heavy fog and the air was chilly, and Sammy Thax was wet from head to heels. But finally they rounded Sudie up and drove her through the gate which they had propped wide open. As she went through, she tossed her head playfully and kicked up her heels. She sure was a frisky cow.

"The devil's daughter, that's what she is," muttered Rindy, closing the gate behind her.

Sammy Thax and his father drove her up the lane and got her headed in the right direction. "I guess you can drive her the rest of the way home by yourself, Sam," said Mr. Milliken. "When you get there, tell Alec Apple I said put a yoke on her. She's the beatin'est cow for jumpin' I ever saw."

As Sammy Thax drove Sudie up the lane, he thought of the rhyme, *"Hey diddle diddle, the cat and the fiddle, the cow jumped over the moon."* If any cow could jump over the moon, he decided, it was Sudie. Gran had taught him that verse and a lot of others when he was just a little kid. He looked back and saw Bowser sneaking along at a safe distance behind him. He called, "Come on, then, you can help me drive her home. But don't bark, you hear me?" Bowser meekly rolled his eyes and didn't make a sound.

In spite of being damp and chilly and hungry, Sammy Thax enjoyed watching the sun come up.

The fog would soon be gone; it would be a fine day. But it was Monday. School. The worst day in the week was Monday. The rail fences on both sides of the lane were covered with honeysuckle and devil's shoestring on which were still a few red trumpets. Frost was late in coming, and a morning glory vine was opening its blue flowers to the sunlight. Sammy Thax thought of Gran. She loved blue morning glories and always kept them growing on the trellis by the well. There were many spider webs beside the road, strung with beads of fog. The big sugar maple near the Apples' springhouse was as yellow as butter. Gran always said that October was the prettiest month.

They were in sight of the Apples' farmhouse, and Sammy Thax tried to hurry Sudie along, but she took her time. She stopped to gaze at tufts of grass beside the road, and where the branch ran across the road, she stopped to drink. Bowser made an impatient lunge at her, but Sammy Thax said, "Let her alone, dog. You get her excited, no telling what she will do."

Mr. Apple saw them coming and hurried to open his big farm gate. He waited beside it, to head Sudie in, and when Sammy Thax got near, he said, "I just found out she was gone. Jumped over into your Pa's cornfield again, I'll be bound."

"Yessir, she did," said Sammy Thax. "Pa said please to put a yoke on her, to stop her from jumping."

"I'm goin' to sell her to the butcher, plague take her," said Mr. Apple. He picked up a clod of dirt and threw it at Sudie. Tossing her head, she sauntered toward the milking pen. "A limb of Satan," muttered Mr. Apple.

The farm bell outside the Apples' kitchen door rang briefly. "That's the breakfast bell," said Mr. Apple. "Have you done had your breakfast, Sam?"

"No, sir, but I'd better get along home," said Sammy Thax.

"Ah, pshaw, eat with us, boy," said Mr. Apple, laying a hand on Sammy Thax's shoulder. "It ain't so late as all that."

Sammy Thax followed him willingly into the kitchen, for Mrs. Apple was a famous cook. "Mrs. Apple Dumpling" would have been a suitable name for her; she was so round and rosy. She said, "Well, I'm sure glad to see you, Sammy. I haven't got a company breakfast, but you won't mind potluck."

Mr. Apple winked at Sammy Thax. "She always scares us into thinking we might have to go hungry, don't she?" Mrs. Apple quickly set a place for Sammy Thax, and when they were all seated and had the blessing, she heaped his plate with fried ham and grits with red ham gravy, scrambled eggs, and hot buttered biscuits. She poured him a big mug of milk. Suddenly she sprang up. "Law, I nearly forgot my coffee cake," she said and brought it from the oven smelling of cinnamon and yeast, and bubbling with brown sugar and hickory nuts. She cut a big square for Sammy Thax. "A boy that's growing fast needs to eat plenty," she said.

"Looks like you've growed two inches lately, Sam," said Mr. Apple.

"And ain't he healthy lookin'?" Mrs. Apple said. "Law, Sam, when you was born, you just weighed three pounds, and we didn't think you could make it. But your Gran went to work on you; she saved your life and no mistake. Have you all heard from her lately?"

Sammy Thax told them they had had two letters and hoped to hear again soon. "She's bound to be homesick way off up there," said Mrs. Apple.

"A better woman never lived than your grandmother, Sam," said Mr. Apple. "When I was young, I had typhoid fever, and if it hadn't been for her, I would'a died."

"She is a born nurse," said Mrs. Apple, putting another square of coffee cake on Sammy Thax's plate.

Sammy Thax said, "That sure was good, Miz

Apple. I better go now."

Mr. and Mrs. Apple followed him to the door. "Come back soon," said Mrs. Apple. "Mercy on us, I forgot to feed Bowser. Wait a minute."

"Ma will feed him," said Sammy Thax. "We better go now. I had a good time."

"Tell your Pa I'll replace the corn Sudie destroyed," said Mr. Apple. "Tell him the next time he sees her, she'll be beefsteak."

Warm, tired out, filled to the brim with good food, Sammy Thax took the short cut home, whistling all the way. His mother met him at the door with a worried frown. "Whatever took you so long?" she scolded. "Eat your breakfast and get ready for school. You are goin' to be late."

"I had my breakfast at Miz Apple's," said Sammy Thax. "I wisht we had coffee cake for breakfast every mornin' like Miz Apple's."

"I don't think you ever go hungry," his mother said shortly. She went back to washing dishes, and Sammy Thax went upstairs to get ready for school. He was thinking that if Gran had been there, she would have said, "I'll get Miz Apple's receipt for coffee cake and make you some." He got quickly into his school clothes, put his books into the satchel, and went downstairs. His mother handed him his lunch box and he said, "Ma, will you feed Bowser?

Miz Apple forgot him." His mother answered. "Yes, I'll feed him. Now hustle along, or you'll be late."

Sammy Thax didn't go by the road that morning; he took a shortcut across the fields. Standing in a deep hollow, close to the creek, was the finest chestnut tree in the county. Some of the burrs had opened, and Sammy Thax decided to gather a few chestnuts. It was fun finding them, and he could always trade them to good advantage at school. He squinted at the sun, uneasy about the time. But if he was tardy, he could tell Miss Effie how he had to help get Sudie out of the cornfield. That would be a good excuse. He kept picking up chestnuts until he had two pockets bulging with them. Then he headed for school at a brisk trot.

When he came in sight of the schoolhouse, he saw that the schoolyard was empty. He was late. Then, to his joy, he saw Brother Pringle, the preacher, drive into the schoolyard and hitch his horse. "Good, good," thought Sammy Thax. "I'll sneak in right behind him, and Miss Effie might not even notice me." He sprinted across the schoolyard and overtook the minister at the foot of the steps.

"Good morning, Samuel," said Mr. Pringle. "We are both a little late, it appears."

Sammy Thax politely opened the door for him, and when he entered, big and tall, Sammy Thax slid

like an eel in behind him, and got to his seat while Miss Effie was shaking hands with the visitor. She tapped on her desk and said, "Boys and girls, Brother Pringle has come to talk to you this morning. I want you to pay strict attention. But first we will all stand and sing 'Good Morning to You.'"

Sammy Thax drew a deep breath and stood up to sing. Miss Effie had not looked at him at all. He felt very lucky. When the minister had finished his talk and gone, Sammy Thax cautiously took the chestnuts out of his pockets and put them on top of his desk. He put books around them to keep them from rolling off. In a minute he felt a gentle touch on his shoulder. He looked around, and Jud's sister, Mary Kate, was smiling and holding a cupped hand against the side of his desk. Sammy Thax picked up some chestnuts to give to her; then he caught Miss Effie's eye on him. He dropped his hands into his lap and gazed out the window. When she turned back to the blackboard, he swung his arm back and under Mary Kate's desk and she grabbed the nuts. A minute later he heard her gnawing at the shell of a chestnut. Sammy Thax turned and whispered, "Wait till recess."

Tub Thompson sat across the aisle from Sammy Thax. He whistled very softly between his teeth to attract Sammy's attention. When Sammy Thax looked at him, Tub held out a hand. Sammy Thax shook his head. Tub then took a fine red winesap apple out of his desk and held it enticingly. Sammy Thax nodded. Tub dropped his pencil in the aisle between them. As Tub bent to get his pencil, Sammy Thax picked up some chestnuts and swiftly exchanged the nuts for the apple. At that moment Miss Effie turned from the blackboard, and Sammy Thax and Tub bent over their geographies.

About five minutes later a wad of paper hit Sammy Thax behind the ear. He looked around. Jim Mehaffey's eyebrows were going up and down. "Chestnuts," he said, without making a sound. Sammy Thax shook his head. Jim held up a sausage biscuit. Sammy Thax shook his head again. Jim fished in his lunch box and held up a small cake of homemade maple sugar. Sammy Thax nodded. Presently he raised his hand for permission to get a drink of water. As he went to the water bucket at the back of the room, he swapped some chestnuts for the maple sugar.

Back at his desk, he picked up his geography again. His mouth watered for the maple sugar, but he decided not to risk taking a bite before recess. Mary Kate dropped a note over his shoulder. It was from Maggie Harkins. It said, "Give me some chestnuts. I'll trade you jam cake." Sammy Thax looked back and nodded at Maggie. So, when the fifth-grade-reader class was called to the recitation bench, Maggie laid a slice of jam cake, wrapped in white paper, on Sammy Thax's desk. He thrust some chestnuts into her apron pocket.

Miss Effie explained they wouldn't have recess that morning because Brother Pringle's visit had used up the time. When noon and lunchtime came, Sammy Thax gathered up the remaining chestnuts and put them in his pocket. He had his apple, his maple sugar, and his jam cake inside his lunch box. The bell tapped, and everyone stood up. Then Miss Effie spoke, in that voice that made Sammy Thax think of the crack of a whip. She said, "Mary Kate Harkins, Tub Thompson, Jim Mehaffey, Maggie Harkins, Samuel Thaxton Milliken, be seated. The rest of you are dismissed."

With sly grins at the unlucky five, the other boys and girls left the room. Miss Effie stood up, tall and stern. "Bring your lunch boxes here," she said, tapping her desk. "Bring every bit of food you've got." One by one they went up and put their lunches on her desk. Sammy Thax came last, put down his lunch box, and offered her the last of his chestnuts. "Keep the chestnuts," she said. "Pass them around. All of you can now eat chestnuts until the bell rings. Chestnuts are very nourishing."

"S" Stands
for Sammy

FOR EVER SO LONG SAMMY THAX HAD WANTED A pocket knife. True, he had a sort of knife, but it was a poor excuse. It was one his father had discarded. The big blade was broken off close to the hinge, and the smaller one was so weak that it bent backward when he tried to cut with it. One reason he had never said much about wanting a better knife was that Gran thought he was too young for one. She said she had known boys who had cut an artery learning to whittle. She said she heard of one boy who fell down with an open knife in his hand, and it killed him. Sammy Thax was willing to risk all of these—if he could just have a new knife.

He certainly didn't want to worry Gran, but it seemed to him that a lot of boys Gran had heard of had died doing things Sammy Thax wanted to do. When he started learning to swim in the swimming hole below Rindy's house, Gran told him about a little boy who drowned in that creek and was washed away and never seen again. When he started riding horseback by himself to the mill, she warned him that a boy she heard of had been thrown off a horse and dragged to death because his foot got hung in the stirrup. Sammy Thax knew Gran worried because she loved him and didn't want him to get hurt. But Jud and the other boys he knew hadn't got drowned or cut or dragged to death. And now Gran wouldn't worry, because she wouldn't know he had a good knife.

"A fellow needs a knife," Sammy Thax explained to his father. "I can't whittle or play mumble peg with my old knife. I can't even sharpen a pencil with it."

"I've got no objection to you having a better knife, Sam," his father said. "Remind me of it next time we go to town. I'll get you one."

Sammy Thax felt pretty certain that his father would get him one of those one-blade knives that cost a quarter. That wasn't the kind he had in mind. Tub Thompson had the kind he wanted. So at recess the next day he touched Tub on the shoulder and beckoned him aside. Tub said, "What's up?"

"Do you want to trade me your knife?" asked Sammy Thax.

"What you got to trade?" asked Tub Thompson suspiciously.

Sammy Thax drew out his old piece of knife. "Huh," snorted Tub, "I reckon you would like to trade me that." He started to walk away.

"Wait," said Sammy Thax, "I was meaning to give you some boot." He drew his slingshot out of his hip pocket. It was an extra good slingshot that Rindy had made for him out of well-seasoned hickory. He reached down and put a pebble in it and sent it singing through the air.

"What else you got?" asked Tub. Sammy Thax drew out a dollar watch. It was a very goodlooking watch. It still had both hands and only one little crack in the crystal. It had a nice fob on it too, a leather fob with a little brass ship attached to the end of it. On the back of it was engraved "Souvenir of Tennessee Centennial." Sammy Thax's father had worn it a long time before he gave it to Sammy Thax. Tub's eyes brightened. He took it in his hand and held it to his ear. "It ain't runnin'," he said. He handed it back. Sammy Thax shook it, and it began to tick. He held it to Tub's ear. "It will run in warm weather," he said. "Any watch, pretty near, quits in cool weather."

Tub said, "What else you got?" Sammy Thax searched frantically in his pockets and brought out two nice agates and a handful of small marbles. "Is that all?" asked Tub with scorn. "Gee, what do you think your old knife is worth?" asked Sammy Thax.

"Where's your compass?" asked Tub. Sadly, Sammy Thax drew his compass out of his inside jacket pocket. He hated to part with it. His Uncle William had been to Cuba in the Spanish-American War and had brought it to him when he came home. Sammy Thax, it is true, never really used it, but it was a pleasure to carry around and show to the boys.

Tub said, "I'll trade you my knife for your agates and your slingshot and your compass. You can keep the marbles and the watch and that old knife."

"It's a deal," said Sammy Thax. Tub pocketed his new possessions and handed over his knife and walked away. Sammy stood still and turned the knife over in his hand. It was just the kind he wanted. He opened the four blades. The hinges were strong and perfect. The blades were sharp. The handle was yellow bone, as slick as glass. On the front side was an S-shaped piece of silver set smoothly into the bone. "I can always prove it's my knife," thought Sammy Thax, grinning: " 'S' stands for Sam."

On the way home from school that afternoon Sammy Thax kept his hand on the knife in his pocket. Now and then he took it out and looked at it and rubbed his thumb across the smooth handle. "It's a jim-dandy, all right," he said to himself. He wanted to show it off at home but then he decided he had better not. His mother might scold him about trading off his compass. She might want him to trade back with Tub. He would just show it to Rindy and get Rindy to make him a new slingshot with it. Rindy would never tell anybody—you could count on him.

When he was nearly home, an idea struck him, such a nice idea that he couldn't wait to get started. He would take his new knife and carve his initials on the big beech tree that grew near the springhouse. It was a very old tree, and over the years a lot of boys had carved initials on it, or sometimes their names. Hester had a beau named Tim Wilson, and one Sunday when he came calling, he and Hester had walked to the springhouse where he had carved a heart on the beech tree bark, and inside the heart he had carved "Tim and Hester." Hester was pleased and showed it to Sammy Thax, but he thought it was silly. All he wanted to do was to cut his own initials, "S.T.M," and when he was as old as Rindy, they would still be there.

He left the road, climbed the rail fence, and cut across the pasture to the springhouse. If Hester or Susan came to get water, they would want to know why he was there. But there was no one in sight, so he put his books and lunch box on a flat rock and got out his knife. He walked all around the beech tree, trying to decide where he wanted to put his initials.

He found a nice smooth spot, just high enough from the ground, and set to work. He tested first one blade and then another and decided on the smallest blade. It was very sharp, with a keen point. He wanted a pretty, curving capital S. He frowned and bit his tongue. It was not as easy as he had thought it would be. Slowly, very slowly he carved the curves. He thought his S was lopsided, but it would do. The T went faster, just two straight lines with pretty little tips like Tim had cut on his T. Now for the M.

A wind had sprung up, and he was getting cold. It was November. He thought about Gran. In every letter she spoke of how cold it was in Idaho. He wished Gran could come home for Thanksgiving. He stood there, lost in thought of Gran and fingering his knife. He murmured, "You need not worry about me cutting myself, Gran." Then he went to work on his M.

He was getting along fine with it, but he was so bent upon his carving that he didn't realize how close his left hand was to the blade. He was nearly done when the knife slipped and cut across the base of his left thumb. It hardly hurt at all, the blade was so sharp. It was only when the blood came streaming out that he realized he had a deep cut. Carefully he wiped the blood off the knife blade onto his pants leg, closed it, and put the knife in his pocket. He went to the horse trough close by and washed his hand, but as fast as he washed it, the blood flowed again. He didn't want to go to the house and have to explain what had happened. His mother might take the knife away from him and never give it back. He didn't have a handkerchief. If he tore off part of his shirttail, his mother wouldn't stop asking until she found out why it was torn.

Then, close against the south wall of the spring-house he saw a tall stalk of mullen, with thick limber leaves still hanging on it. He pulled off some and pressed them against the cut. That helped a lot. It was near sundown, and he knew he must be getting to the house. All the way up the hill he kept the leaves pressed tight against the cut. He had forgotten his books and lunch box. As he went indoors, he shoved his hand, leaves and all, into his jacket pocket. His mother was in the kitchen bending over

the oven. The kitchen smelled deliciously of yeast and cinnamon. "Is that you, Sam?" his mother called over her shoulder. "You are awful late. Been gathering chestnuts, I reckon. Are you hungry?"

"No'm," said Sammy Thax, making for the back stairs that led up from the kitchen.

"Been eating pawpaws and persimmons, I guess," said his mother. "Well, I made a coffee cake. Miz Apple was by here and wrote off her receipt."

Sammy Thax hurried on to his room. He hid the knife in the tin box holding his valuables. Then he took a clean handkerchief and held it tightly around the cut, which was still oozing blood. He felt sort of dizzy and tired, so lay down across his bed. He meant to get up in a few minutes, but he fell asleep and did not wake until his mother shook him by the shoulder and said, "Wake up, Sam. Supper's ready. Are you sick?"

"No, Ma, I'm not sick. Leave me alone," mumbled Sammy Thax. His mother put down her lighted lamp on a table by the bed. "My stars, Sam, you've hurt your hand. It's bled a spot on the bed. How did you come to do it?"

"Aw, Ma, it don't hurt," said Sammy Thax. "It's just a scratch."

"Scratch, my foot," said Ma. "Let me get the turpentine and some cloth to bandage it." She went downstairs and very quickly came back with a bottle of turpentine and a strip of old pillow slip. She soaked the cut and neatly bandaged it. "There," she said, "you cut that on a knife, didn't you?" Sammy Thax said, "Yes'm."

"Whose knife have you been fooling with?" she demanded. Sammy Thax thought the jig was up. Then he said, "It's a real sharp knife Tub got for Christmas last year."

"Well, from now on let him keep his knife in his pocket and use your own. It ain't sharp enough to hurt you." She headed toward the back stairs, and Sammy Thax followed. He glanced back toward his bureau. Cut or no cut, he was proud of his trade with Tub.

Bowser's Lost

IT WAS ALMOST THANKSGIVING, BUT SAMMY Thax did not feel the least bit like giving thanks. He had seen the big, fat tom turkey cooling in the springhouse, ready to be cooked. In the pantry he had seen a row of pies, mince and apple, pumpkin and chess, that Ma had baked. He knew the attic was stored with chestnuts and hickory nuts and black walnuts and wine sap apples and sugar pears because he had helped gather all of them. He knew that down in the cellar the shelves were filled with jars of preserves and pickles and canned fruits and vegetables, and that sweet potatoes and turnips were stored in straw in a separate room. He knew that the smoke house was filled with good smoked hams and pork shoulders hanging from the rafters, and slabs of bacon and sacks of sausage. All those good things, and still Sammy Thax was moping around like a sick puppy.

For one reason, Gran was not there. Lots of other relatives were coming for Thanksgiving, but Gran was way off in Idaho. He had rather have had Gran come home than all the other relatives put together. For another reason, Bowser was lost. He had been lost since the past Monday. Monday afternoon he had gone with Sammy Thax, as usual, to bring up the cows to be milked. He had been there at suppertime, and Sammy Thax had fed him. But the next morning when Sammy Thax had started out very early to see if he had caught anything in his traps, he had whistled and called, but Bowser had not come. Sammy Thax had felt lonely and a little worried as he started off to the woods alone, but he thought, "He must be over at the Apples', playing with Sport." The two muskrats in Sammy's traps had cheered him up.

When he got home from school that afternoon and no shaggy brown dog with long, flopping ears ran to meet him and to jump up and lick his face, Sammy Thax began to feel scared. He whistled and called, loud and long. He went to all his traps, to be sure Bowser hadn't got caught in one of them. He went to the barn where his father and Rindy were mending harness and asked if they had seen Bowser all day, but they hadn't. Tears stung Sammy Thax's eyes as he turned away. "Somebody stole him, I bet," he muttered, "or maybe poisoned him." But Bowser was a good dog; he never sucked eggs or chased chickens; he never bit anybody or killed a sheep.

Sammy Thax turned around, put his head inside the harness room door, and said, "I want to ride Old Ned around and look for Bowser. He might be hurt."

"Well, go ahead," his father said. "Ned's in the back stall, eatin' hay."

"That dog, he mos' likely be home 'bout suppertime, Sam," reassured Rindy. But Sammy Thax couldn't wait for suppertime. He saddled Old Ned and rode off. First he rode to the Apples.' When he knocked at the back door, Mrs. Apple opened it. Her broad, rosy face broke into a smile. "Well, come in, Sammy," she said. "I've got a jam cake right out of the oven. You must of smelled it cookin'."

"I can't come in, Miz Apple," said Sammy Thax. "I'm huntin' for Bowser. Have you seen him? He's been gone since last night."

Her jolly face turned solemn. "Bowser is lost?" she said in distress. "Oh, my, I sure hope you find him. But he hasn't been on the place that I know of. If he shows up, we'll let you know right straight."

"Thank you, Miz Apple," said Sammy Thax forlornly. He mounted Old Ned and rode off. He started next to Jud's house, then he remembered that the whole family had gone to Dover to spend Thanksgiving with Jud's grandmother. He rode from farm to farm and stopped at the Thompsons', the Mehaffeys', the Reeds', the Simpsons', the Hoffstetters'. No one had seen Bowser.

It was getting dark when he headed home. He didn't feel hungry. Instead, he felt hollow and lonely and cold when Ma met him at the kitchen door. She patted his shoulder and said, "Don't worry so; he will turn up. And if he don't, you've got Domino. He is a real smart pup." Ma didn't understand that no dog could take Bowser's place. Not even Domino.

The next morning still no Bowser. At school that day, Sammy Thax couldn't get his mind on his lessons. Miss Effie dismissed school a little early because the next day was Thanksgiving, and Sammy Thax hurried home, in hopes Bowser might be there.

He met his mother coming up from the springhouse with the big turkey gobbler, ready for the oven, in her arms. "He weighs all of twenty-five pounds," she said. "Ain't it nice that Uncle William

101

and Aunt Maude are comin' for dinner? We are goin' to have a real nice Thanksgivin'."

Sammy Thax knew she was trying to cheer him up. But how could any day be a big day with Gran gone and Bowser lost? He went to the woods, whistling and calling, but no Bowser came.

Next morning the house was filled with delicious smells of roasting turkey and chestnut stuffing, homemade rolls, coffee, and spices. Fires blazed in every fireplace. The long white tablecloth was spread on the dining table; the last of the yellow chrysanthemums were in a bowl in the center. Hester and Susan were all dressed up, and his mother made Sammy Thax put on his Sunday best. About noon Uncle William, Aunt Maude, and their three sons drove up in their new surrey. Usually Sammy Thax was overjoyed when they came, but today he hung back and kept to himself as much as possible.

Late in the afternoon when the big dinner was over and the company had gone, it began to snow— big, lazy flakes at first, then faster and faster until the air was white. "Looks like we are in for a real wintertime snow," grumbled Mr. Milliken, as he pulled on his boots to go to the barn. Usually Sammy Thax hollered for joy when it snowed, for then he and Bowser went rabbit hunting. But that evening as he pulled on his "hand-me-down" jacket and cap to bring in stove wood, he paid no attention to the snow except to wonder if Bowser was hurt and if he would freeze to death that night. Sammy had given up hope of finding Bowser.

He had his big armload of wood and was starting toward the house when he saw a strange man driving up in a rickety buggy, pulled by a bony horse. Just as the buggy drew up to the back gate, Mr. Milliken came up from the barn and said, "Good evening. Is there something I can do for you?" Sammy Thax was curious, and he waited to see what the stranger wanted. The man bent forward and lifted a worn, old buggy rug which had covered the floor of his buggy. "Reckon this here dog is you all's?" he asked. "I heard from Rindy that your boy was lookin' for a lost dog."

Sammy Thax dropped the stove wood and sprang to the side of the buggy. He took a quick look, and his voice rang out, shrill with joy and excitement, "Pa, it's him. It's Bowser." He lifted the dog and held him in his arms. Bowser whined and licked his face, his hands, and his jacket. He was shivering all over, and one eye was swollen shut. One foreleg was bandaged with a rag. Sammy Thax kept saying over and over, "Good old Bowser, where have you been? Good dog." He turned to the stranger and said, "Where did you find him?"

"He come to my house las' night, in the night," said the man. "He must'a been in a turrible fight, or some kind'er accident. His leg is broke—I set it the best I could. I'm pretty fair at doctorin' animals, but he needs a lot more doctorin' yet."

"He'll get plenty from Sam," Mr. Milliken said. "Won't you come in and let my wife give you some supper? It's a rough night to be out, and we sure are much obliged to you. I'd like to pay you for your trouble."

"Sho'," said the man, "I wouldn't take no money. But my wife, she's got a new baby, 'bout a week old, and poorly." He glanced at the big pail of foaming fresh milk Mr. Milliken was carrying. "If you could spare a drap of milk?"

"Of course we can, all you want," said Mr. Milliken. "Get out and hitch your horse. Let's get in out of this snow." The man obeyed, and when they entered the warm, cheerful kitchen, Sammy Thax was there before them hand-feeding Bowser with scraps of turkey and dressing. His mother was heating a pan of milk for the dog.

She turned and looked closely at the strange man. "Ain't you Josh Adams?" she asked.

"That's right," he answered. "I'm Rindy Adams' cousin."

"Well, bless my soul," cried Mrs. Milliken,

"I'm glad to see you, Josh. Didn't you marry Melly Harper?"

"Yes'm, that's right," he said.

"And didn't Rindy tell me you all have a big family?" she asked.

"This new one, a week old, well he makes seven," he said proudly.

"Well, you've done met my husband and son," Mrs. Milliken said, bustling around to set a plate for him. "We had a big dinner, and there's plenty left. I'm going to fix you a plate to eat while I pack a basket for Melly and the children." She put a heaping plate of food before the man and a cup of steaming coffee. While he ate, she filled a gallon jug with fresh milk. Then into a split basket she put a pan of rolls, a mince pie, half a jam cake, some sliced ham and turkey and a jar of peach pickle.

She lighted the lantern and said, "Here, Sam, the dog is alright. Leave him be and run down cellar and get Josh a bag of sweet potatoes." Sammy Thax gave Bowser a loving pat and whispered, "He's asleep." When he got back from the cellar with the potatoes, he hurried up to the attic and brought down a basket of apples and chestnuts.

When Josh got up to go, he said, "We didn't have much of a dinner at my house today, but we will feast tomorrow. I thank you kindly."

"We thank you, Josh," said Mrs. Milliken. "This boy has moped around the blessed time the dog's been gone."

"You were mighty kind to bring him home on a night such as this," Mr. Milliken added. "We won't forget it. Here, Sam, light him to the gate with the lantern."

Sammy Thax helped Josh get the food and milk stowed into the buggy. Then he reached up to shake his hand and said, "If your dog ever gets lost, well, let me know. I'll sure try to help you find him."

The Special Christmas Tree

ONE VERY COLD SATURDAY MORNING ABOUT THE middle of December the Milliken family was eating breakfast in the big, comfortable kitchen. "Here it is two weeks till Christmas, and we haven't got a Christmas tree, Pa," complained Susan. Mr. Milliken finished his second cup of coffee and looked at Sammy Thax. "How about it, Sam?" he asked. "You want to help me get one in this mornin'?"

"You all will freeze, Pa," said Hester. "There was ice on the water bucket this mornin'."

"It's an inch thick on the pond," said Mr. Milliken. "This has been about as cold a December as I can remember. But it is goin' to be colder by night;

the wind is square out of the north. What you say, Sam?"

"I'll get my jacket," said Sammy Thax as he walked upstairs and put on his heavy jacket and the old red stocking cap Gran had knitted for him. Usually getting in the Christmas tree was one of the best things that happened in the whole year, but this year was different. Sammy Thax did not feel excited. Nevertheless, he joined his father and a still limping Bowser.

Mr. Milliken shouldered the ax, and Sammy Thax dragged his homemade sled behind them, to bring the tree home on. They headed for the rocky cedar glade near the creek in the back pasture. The frozen ground crunched under their heavy shoes as they walked, and the horse trough was rimmed with long icicles. The north wind rattled the tin roof on the barn and bent the cedar trees. Mr. Milliken's long, thin nose turned blue with the cold. He said, "Sam, I sure hope you get some fun out of this Christmas tree cutting. It's kind of a tough job any kind of weather, but a day like this, well it makes you wish Christmas come in July. It's goin' to zero tonight, I'm certain."

"Rindy could have cut it," said Sammy Thax. "He cut it last year."

"He has got a terrible cold," said Mr. Milliken.

"This wind would give him pneumonia. You pick a tree you like now, and be quick about it."

"I've done picked one, Pa," said Sammy Thax. "Gran and me picked one out back in July." It was true. He and Gran had been picking blackberries together that day in the brierpatch near the glade, and while they were resting in the shade, Gran had pointed out a lovely cedar tree, a perfect cone, that stood a little apart from the others. "Look, Sam," Gran had said, "there's a Christmas tree that's what you might call perfect. Growin' off to itself thata'way, it has rounded the same on all sides. Where a tree is crowded like, it gets lopsided."

Later on, just before Gran went to Idaho, she and Sammy Thax were hunting a turkey hen and her poults, and she had noticed the tree again and said, "There's that pretty Christmas tree, Sam. I hope you get it this year. It will touch the ceilin'." And Sammy Thax had said, "I will, Gran."

So, that icy morning, Sammy Thax ran to the tree and laid his hand on the trunk and said, "This is the one we picked." "Well, it's a beauty," Mr. Milliken said, "and loaded with blue cedar berries. Your Gran always did love them blue berries; she said they was as pretty to her as red holly berries. I almost hate to cut it. But if you and Gran picked it, cut it I will."

He swung his ax, which Rindy had sharpened just the day before, and after a few, hard strokes the tall beautiful cedar shuddered and swayed and came crashing down. Bowser was so excited that he barked loudly and ran around on three legs, sniffing the tree. "Looks like Bowser is gettin' more fun out of this than you and me, Sam," said Mr. Milliken as he and Sammy Thax loaded the tree onto the sled.

"I'm havin' fun, Pa," said Sammy Thax quietly. His father slipped a strong stick through the end of the rope, to make a sort of double-tree, and they pulled together. It wasn't easy, dragging the sled uphill over the uneven ground, and when they got as far as the woodpile, Mr. Milliken was panting. He said, "Phew, Sam, I'm near frozen solid." He wiped his watering eyes and nose. "Let's go indoors and thaw out a spell and get Ma to give us some hot coffee before we do any more."

Inside the warm kitchen Sammy Thax took off his gloves and rubbed his hands together. They were so cold that they began to ache. "Here, Sam," his mother said, "put your hands in this pan of water; it's barely warm. It's no fitten day to be worryin' with a Christmas tree. Sometimes I think a big old tree is more trouble than it's worth."

"Ma, how can you say such a thing?" cried

Susan. "A cedar tree makes the whole house smell like Christmas." She poured a big cup of coffee and served it to her father. "Yes, and when it comes down on New Year's Eve, it sheds all over the parlor rug and takes me all day to clean up," grumbled Mrs. Milliken.

"I'll clean it up, Ma," said Susan, as she handed Sammy Thax a cup of hot apple cider. "That's what you say now," said Mrs. Milliken, briskly shoving stove wood into the firebox by the stove. "But when the time comes, it generally falls to my lot to clean up."

Mr. Milliken finished his coffee and stood up. "Come on, Sam, let's finish our job," he said. They went to the toolshed and got the bucksaw and sawed the tree squarely and smoothly off just below the bottom branches. Then Mr. Milliken nailed into place the stout, square wooden base they used every year. He braced the tree firmly from the four sides. "There," he said. "It's ready for the parlor, and it won't topple over." Together they dragged the tree indoors and set it up in the usual place, the north corner of the parlor, farthest from the fireplace.

Mrs. Milliken and the girls watched them. "Law, Pa, it's the prettiest tree we've ever had," said Hester, touching it proudly. Susan agreed and added,

"I wish Gran was here to bake the little cakes to hang on it."

"She was a great hand for making them little German cakes, wasn't she?" said Mrs. Milliken. "She would work on 'em daylight to dark, bakin' angels and flowers and stars and what all for the tree. And Sam, you mind how you would put in them little wires to hang 'em up by, before they was baked?"

Sammy Thax was silent. He was thinking what fun it was when he and Gran worked on the little cakes and how they would pop a dishpan full of popcorn and string it in long, white garlands for the tree. Then Gran would take clean wheat straw and make little dolls two or three inches high to hang on the tree. She told him that her grandmother came from Germany and had taught her how to make the cakes and dolls.

Just then there was a knock at the front door, and Susan darted to the hall to see who it might be. Her mother followed. At the front door, shivering in the cold wind, stood Mr. Henry Henderson, holding a neat black case. "Good morning, ladies," he said; "I've come to deliver the pictures I took a while back."

"Well, come in," said Mrs. Milliken. "I had about give you out."

"I'm sorry I have been so long," he answered,

following her and Susan into the cold parlor. "My wife was sick for weeks, and I couldn't do much work on pictures. But I think you will like what I've got here."

Mrs. Milliken said, "This is my husband, Mr. Henderson, and this is Hester and Susan, my daughters. And you remember Sam. Let's go to the family room where it's warm." She led the way down the hall to the big old room where good, comfortable split-bottom chairs with red cushions were placed before a roaring log fire.

"My, this is cheerful," said Mr. Henderson warming his cold hands before the fire. "Now, let's see what you all think of my work." He opened the black case, made of pasteboard, and lifted out a life-sized picture of Sammy Thax, seated. The flowered velvet looked pretty in the picture, and it was tinted. So also was Sammy Thax tinted—hair, eyes, clothes—very true to life. The family stood before the picture, looking at it and struck dumb with admiration. Finally Mr. Milliken said, "It's a speakin' likeness." Mrs. Milliken nodded and wiped tears from her eyes with a corner of her apron.

"It shows how nice you can look, Sam, when you fix up," said Susan reproachfully. Hester added, "I wish Gran could see it."

Quickly Mr. Henderson took from the case a

smaller copy of the same picture, also tinted. "It was my understanding you wanted a smaller one for the grandmother's family album," he said. "The tinting is a little extra, but well worth it, I'm sure you'll agree."

"Well worth it," agreed Mrs. Milliken, who usually drove a hard bargain. "If his Gran don't get any other present this year, she won't complain. This boy is the apple of her eye."

"No wonder. He's a fine boy," beamed Mr. Henderson. Sammy gave him a sour look. He did not believe Mr. Henderson meant a word he said.

Sunday morning at breakfast Mrs. Milliken said, "Well, if we aim to get that picture of Sam and that album off to Gran in time for Christmas, we'd better pack it after church."

"No church today, Ma," said Susan. "Don't you know this is third Sunday, not first."

"What am I thinkin' of?" exclaimed Mrs. Milliken. "Well, let's pack Gran's gift this mornin', and Pa, you'll have to take it to the express office tomorrow." She looked around the table. "Has anybody else got anything to send to Gran?" she asked. "It's the first Christmas she has not been here, and she might feel sort'a lonesome."

"I'm going to send her the two pillow slips I made for my hope chest," said Susan.

"Have you give up hope, Sue?" teased her father.

Susan tossed her head and ran to her room. When she came back, she brought the two pillow slips, edged with lace she had crocheted. "Gran will think too much of them ever to use them, I bet," said her mother.

"I made five yards of tatting last summer," said Hester. "Gran loves to trim her collars and cuffs with tatting. I'm going to send it to her."

Mrs. Milliken slipped Sammy Thax's picture into the big album and marked the place with a red ribbon. She wrapped it carefully first in tissue paper, then in newspaper. Mr. Milliken stood by watching. Then he wiped his eyes and blew his nose and said, "I'll send Gran and Minnie a nice big ham. Gran thought ham was better than turkey any day." He went to the smokehouse to get it.

When he came back, he brought the ham, hickory-smoked and aged for a year. He also brought a good-sized pine box with a lid. "Here's a good box for packin' everything in," he said. "It's that box the sausage grinder was shipped in last year. I stored it in the smokehouse."

"It's the very thing we need!" Mrs. Milliken said. "And plenty of room for everything. I'm goin' to put in a jar of damson preserves for Gran; them's her favorite kind, a jar of blackberry jam too, for the children."

Everyone but Sammy Thax had a hand in packing that box, and it was well packed. He just stood and watched. But just before the lid was put on he said, "Wait, Pa." He ran to the parlor and with his good sharp knife he cut a beautiful bough, loaded with blue berries, from the Christmas tree. He hurried back and laid it on top of everything else.

"Is that your present to Gran?" scoffed Susan. "I don't call that much of a present."

Mr. Milliken looked at Sammy Thax and saw him blinking back the tears. "I have a notion Gran will be mighty pleased to get that piece of cedar," he said. "Her and Sam picked out that tree together last summer." So saying, he set the lid in place, lifted his hammer, and nailed it down, and Gran's box was ready to go.

A Store-Bought
Valentine

Saint valentine's day was just two weeks away, and Sammy Thax was worried. With his elbow on his desk, he propped his chin in his palm and gazed out the window at the fast-falling rain. He had never before been worried about a valentine. He had always thought valentines were silly, and he had teased Jud and the other boys who put them in the school post office on Valentine's Day. But that was before Miriam Mason had started to school at Greenglade.

Her father, Mr. Will Mason, had a hardware store in Richfield. He also had a farm and had recently built a nice house on it and moved out from

119

town. So in January Miriam had entered the country school. Sammy Thax turned his head to look at her as she stood at the blackboard working an arithmetic problem. Beside her, working another problem, stood Jud's sister, Mary Kate. Mary Kate's hair hung down her back in two thick brown plaits, with ribbon bows at the end of each. But Miriam's hair, the color of corn silks, hung down her back in curls. Mary Kate wore a neat, dark, brown woolen dress, and a brown- and white-checked pinafore. But Miriam's dress was rose-colored challis, printed all over in little blue roses. Sammy Thax sighed deeply. Mary Kate was pretty enough, and Gran had liked her. Gran said she was very ladylike and mannerly to old people. But Miriam was the prettiest girl he had ever seen.

Lots of the other boys thought so too. They were always showing off at recess, if Miriam was around, by standing on their heads, walking on their hands, jumping over a pole held high by other boys, wiggling their ears, or bragging about how much they could lift. Sammy Thax didn't show off for her, but he wanted to give her a beautiful valentine. He knew she would get lots of other valentines, but if he could give her the prettiest one, maybe she would be his sweetheart. Last year Hester's beau had given her one that was very large and lacy with a red heart in the center. Sammy Thax wanted one like that for Miriam.

The two girls finished their problems and returned to their desks. As Mary Kate passed Sammy Thax, she gave him a shy sweet smile. He knew she liked him better than any other boy in school. She was smart, and sometimes she worked his arithmetic problems for him. Miriam passed by without a glance in his direction. Instead she smiled and fluttered her fingers in a sort of wave to Jesse Watson. It made Sammy Thax mad. Jesse was the biggest showoff in school. He was very conceited. He parted his hair in the middle and wore neckties to school, which no other boy did. His father was the county judge, and Jesse bragged that when he got grown, he was going to be a senator. Sammy Thax didn't see how a girl could stand Jesse.

The next day was Saturday, and Sammy Thax had to chop stove wood all morning. At noontime it began to rain, and his father said, "You can't chop any more wood today, that's certain, but I tell you what you can do. You can go to the barn and help Rindy shell seed corn. He knows how to pick the best ears."

Sammy Thax loved Rindy, and when they got settled to work in the snug corn crib with rain drumming down on the roof, he felt good. He liked the dry, musty smell of the corncrib, mixed with the good animal smells from the shed where Old Ned and Bossy and Samson were standing, munching hay. Bowser lay at his feet. Except that one leg was a little shorter than the others, Bowser was as good as new. And Domino was a beautiful pup now, but Bowser was jealous of him. Sammy Thax gave Bowser a pat, then he said, turning red, "Rindy, if you was a boy and you needed some money real bad, to buy something, how would you get it?"

"Well now, lemme see," said Rindy, scratching his grizzled head, "this time of year 'bout the best way I know is to trap. It's a little late in the winter, but it's been so cold I think the skins is still prime."

"But I haven't had any luck trappin' lately," said Sammy Thax. "I haven't caught a single varmint in three weeks."

"I tell you what," said Rindy. "You know where the big old chestnut tree stands in the hollow?" Sammy Thax nodded. "Well, I was passin' there yestiddy," Rindy went on, "and I saw what looked to me like the entrance to a polecat den. It's near the old cedar stump, real close by the big chestnut. The ground is wore plumb slick, like as if the varmints been comin' in and out lately. If it is a den of polecats there, they'll 'bout clean up your Ma's young chickens this spring."

"What's a skunk skin worth now, Rindy?" asked Sammy Thax.

"About fifty cents for a short stripe, they tell me, if the skin is prime," Rindy answered. Carefully he selected two more big yellow ears of corn and handed them to Sammy Thax to shell. As he shelled his own ears, he said, "Did I ever tell you 'bout the time a Confederate soldier was hidin' in that deep hollow?" Sammy Thax shook his head and said eagerly, "Tell me."

"Well, it was after the bad battle at Hartsville," Rindy said, "and this here young soldier was wounded, but not serious. He could still travel. His folks lived over yonder where the Harkins live now. He was tryin' to get home, poor fellow. He saw two Yankee soldiers comin', and he hid in the hollow, but they found him anyhow, and they told him he got to surrender and go to prison. Well, he said he ain't goin' to surrender. Anyhow, he drawed his gun and killed one of 'em, and the other Yankee, well he killed that poor boy. And they do say that when that time of year comes, if you down in the hollow, you can see his ghost and hear him moan."

Sammy Thax had stopped shelling corn to listen. His eyes were big and round, and he asked, almost in a whisper, "Do you reckon it's true, Rindy? Do you believe in ghosts?"

"Yes, I do, boy," said the old man. "There's a heap we don't understand that goes on in this world. I know I've seen ghosts in my time, but I never did see that soldier ghost."

It was getting toward dark when they finished shelling the seed corn. The rain had stopped. On his way out of the barn Sammy Thax opened the door of the harness room and took down a steel trap from a hook on the wall. Rindy grinned. He chuckled, "looks like you're goin' to set your trap tonight, boy. Well, that's best. You wouldn't want to set no trap on the Lord's day."

Sammy Thax hesitated. He wanted very much to ask Rindy to go with him for fear of the soldier's ghost. But Rindy would think he was a coward. So he called Bowser, and the two of them set out toward the hollow. A chill wind blew out of the north—the sky was heavy with clouds. Sammy Thax went briskly enough across the open meadow, but as he approached the wooded hollow, his feet lagged. Bowser bristled and growled low in his throat, and Sammy Thax said, "Shut up, dog. You act like you had seen a ghost. Stay here now, and don't bark or anything."

Half running, half sliding, he scrambled down the steep slope into the hollow. It was getting so dark down there he could hardly find the cedar stump

124

and the entrance to the skunks' den. When he did, he set his trap as quickly as he could and covered it completely with dead chestnut leaves. Then, with his heart beating like a big bass drum, he started up the steep side of the hollow. The wind nearly blew him backward, and behind him he heard an awful sound, a low whining moan, and a sound like wings. He scrambled on up the steep slope, and when he looked back over his shoulder, he saw a lot of crows settling for the night in the chestnut tree. He yelled, "Come on, Bowser," and took to his heels. He ran all the way home, and when he got to the back gate, he almost fell into Rindy who was coming through the gate with a gallon can of coal oil in his hand.

"Good land, boy," cried Rindy, "you 'bout knocked me over. What's the matter? Ghost chase you? T'aint time of year for him. I shouldn't a'told you that tale."

Sunday morning Sammy Thax wanted very much to go to his trap, but he knew his father would not like it. Once he had asked Gran if it was a sin to go to your traps on Sunday, and she had said, "Ain't six days a week enough for trappin', Sammy? I guess the Lord understands how a boy feels about his traps, but if I was you, I'd wait till tomorrow."

Sammy waited, though he thought it was the longest Sunday ever. And Monday morning he had to help with the milking and feeding because Rindy was sick, so he didn't get to visit his trap until he was on his way to school. As he approached the hollow in the bright morning sunlight, he didn't feel scared at all. He scrambled down the steep slope and cautiously made his way to where he had set his trap. Then he gave a gasp and whispered, "Got him!"

Sure enough, a fine, short stripe skunk was caught by one leg in the trap. With a long, heavy stick Sammy Thax hit him one fatal blow on the head. Then he removed him from the trap and hid him in a hollow log. After school he would skin him. A strong odor of skunk was everywhere, but Sammy Thax didn't think it would cling to him. He stopped at the branch that crossed the road and washed his hands with sand and the cold running water. He thought the brisk wind would get rid of any other odor.

But when he entered the schoolroom, which was well warmed by the big stove, Tub Thompson grabbed his nose, and some of the girls began to giggle. Miss Effie opened a window and said, "Seems like Samuel Thaxton has been trapping." Miriam whispered something behind her hand to Susan Duncan, and they got permission to move their seats nearer to the stove and farther from Sammy

Thax. But Mary Kate, who sat just behind him, did not move. Tears of sympathy brimmed in her brown eyes, and as she passed his desk to go to her first recitation, she laid an apple on it.

When Saturday finally came, Sammy Thax was allowed to ride to town on the farm wagon with Rindy. Rindy examined the skunk skin which had been stretched on the side of the barn all week and said, "It's prime and you liable to get a good price." When they got to town, he drove first to the produce house and went in with Sammy Thax to see that he wasn't cheated. The man said he had seen better skins, but he would take it for fifty cents. Rindy nodded slightly, and Sammy closed the deal.

He didn't want Rindy to know what he was going to buy. He told him to go ahead to the hardware store and he would be there in a few minutes. When Rindy drove off, he hurried to Mehaffey's Soda Fountain. He had heard Jud say they had the prettiest valentines. Mr. Mehaffey was behind the counter, a very neat, precise little man with a mouth and chin that made Sammy Thax think of a rabbit's. He said, "Good morning, Sam. I haven't seen you for quite a while. What's for you today?"

"A valentine," mumbled Sammy Thax, turning red.

"You've come to the right place," said Mr.

Mehaffey. "We've got a full line, and they are beauties. Let me show you." He led the way to a rack near the front window that was filled with valentines, some for five cents, some ten, some twenty-five, but most of them cost only a penny. None of them were as pretty as Hester's. Disappointed, Sammy Thax turned to leave.

"Hold on," said Mr. Mehaffey. "if it's for your best girl, you might like this one." From a shelf above the rack he lifted down a thin, square fancy box. He lifted the lid, and inside was the most beautiful valentine Sammy Thax had ever seen. It was made of pink paper lace, with gold roses here and there, and a gold Cupid shooting a gold arrow at a red heart in the center. Underneath was a verse

O, please be mine, . .
For I am thine;
Unless you will,
I shall repine.
Be my divine, sweet valentine.

"And look at this," said Mr. Mehaffey. He folded back the heart, and under it was a little handkerchief of thin China silk. Sammy Thax swallowed hard. "How much?" he asked.

"Sixty-five cents," said Mr. Mehaffey, "and cheap for a dollar."

"I haven't got but fifty," said Sammy Thax, turning to leave. He looked so downhearted that Mr. Mehaffey closed the lid and handed him the box, saying, "Take it for fifty, Sam."

"Gee, thanks, Mr. Mehaffey," said Sammy Thax, his face shining.

When he got home, he sneaked his valentine up to his room and hid it in his bottom bureau drawer. He wished Gran could see it, but even if she had been there, he wouldn't have shown it to her or mentioned Miriam. He sharpened his pencil and took out his valentine and penciled "S. T. M." under the verse. And then he decided that on Saturday he would go to the beech tree and cut Miriam's initials beside his, with a heart enclosing both of them.

As they entered the schoolhouse together the morning of Valentine's day, Miriam smiled at him. She glanced at the package in his hand and dimpled. She murmured, "Don't you want to carry my books home for me this afternoon?" Sammy Thax gulped and said yes. More than anything he wanted to walk home with Miriam and carry her books. Several boys had done that, Jesse more often than the others, but Sammy Thax had not had the nerve to ask for the privilege. Walking on air, he followed Miriam into the schoolroom. He dropped his valentine into the decorated box marked "Post Office," beside Miss Effie's desk.

As the hours dragged by, he wondered if the day would ever end. But finally, finally, classes were over, and Miss Effie said, "It's time now for our valentine mail to be distributed. Since Mary Kate has made the highest grades in school this year so far, I'm going to let her be the postmistress."

Mary Kate went to the front and opened the postoffice. She drew out the first valentine and read the name, "Miriam Mason." Sammy Thax's heart skipped a beat. With a pleased smile, Miriam tripped up to receive it. Sammy Thax saw with relief that it was a small one, maybe a penny one. One after another, Mary Kate brought out the valentines, and though no one was left out, Miriam's name was called more often than anyone else's. When finally his own pink box was lifted out, Sammy Thax turned red to the roots of his hair. Jesse jeered, "What's the matter, Sam?" The other boys and girls stared at him, and Miss Effie rapped with her ruler to silence the giggles. Miriam swished back to her seat, opened the box, and clasped her hands in admiration. She gave Sammy Thax a smile that was reward enough for being scared half to death by the soldier's ghost and for smelling like a skunk all one day.

131

"And here's the last one," said Mary Kate. She drew out a red satin heart-shaped box, as big as a dinner plate, and read the name, "Miriam Mason." Miriam went forward and claimed it and opened it then and there. She tilted it a little so the contents could be seen, and a little ripple of "Oh's" filled the room. No one had ever seen such pretty candy. Bonbons in pale pink and green and yellow, like flowers made of sugar, filled the box. Miriam offered it first to Miss Effie, then to Mary Kate, and each took a piece. She then replaced the lid and returned to her seat.

When school was dismissed, Sammy Thax saw Miriam carelessly stuff his valentine into her satchel with the others. But she carried the red satin heart in her hands. He waited outside the school door, but when she came out, Jesse was beside her, carrying her satchel. She leaned toward Sammy Thax and murmured, "Tomorrow you can carry them."

"Well, I won't," said Sammy Thax curtly. To himself he muttered, "I'll never carry them, not if she drops dead." He pulled his cap over his eyes, turned up his coat collar against the stinging wind, and headed for home. Far down the road ahead of him he saw Mary Kate trudging along in a brown coat and a brown hood. He muttered, "If I had had any sense, I'd have give my valentine to her. Next year I'll give her a red satin heart so big it will make Jesse's look like a chigger."

He quickened his steps, and when he overtook Mary Kate, he said brusquely, "Here, lemme carry your books." She looked up at him, and then her long lashes dropped to hide her joy. "Well, thank you, Sammy Thax," she said, and handed her books to him.

Spring Cleaning
Brings Surprises

IT WAS THE FIRST DAY OF MAY AND THE LAST DAY of school, a warm, bright day, the air sweet with the smell of locust trees in bloom. At noon Miss Effie said, "We will have no more lessons today." Then, as there was an excited stir among her pupils, she said firmly, "Keep your seats. After you eat your lunches, you will remain until the usual time this afternoon. But instead of lessons we will clean up our schoolhouse and schoolyard, so it will all be in nice order this fall. Remember, boys and girls, cleanliness is next to godliness." She was always saying that, Sammy thought.

She placed two empty bushel baskets near her

desk and explained that the one on the left was for the girls to put wastepaper in, the one on the right for boys. "Clean your desks thoroughly," she said; "leave no wastepaper and no crumbs of food to attract mice." When all the desks were emptied, Miss Effie inspected them. "Very good," she said. "Now the girls will help me wash windows and blackboards, and sweep the floor, and polish the stove. You boys will go outside and clean the schoolyard. In the far back corner, near the hitching rail, pile all the trash and wastepapers, and we will burn them. You will find a rake outside. I will light the fire when the time comes."

Everyone set to work, indoors and out. To Sammy Thax the afternoon went much faster than it ever did when school was in session. At closing time, Miss Effie tapped the bell, and the boys and girls resumed their seats. She thanked them for the nice job they had done and gave them a little talk about how to improve each shining hour of summer, and then she dismissed them. She stood at the door and shook hands with each boy and girl, nineteen in all, as they passed out the door. Miss Effie was a good teacher. Sammy Thax knew that, and he sort of liked her, especially on the last day of school.

But he was so glad to be on the way home;

with the long summer ahead of him he wanted to toss his books into the air. He wanted to turn hand springs. Now he and Jud could go fishing and swimming in old Bledsoe Creek. And when they weren't working for their fathers, they could explore those caves up near Kentucky and climb the hills around Bethpage and swing on grapevine swings. Summer was the best time of year, Gran always said.

At the thought of Gran his face grew solemn. Gran had been gone pretty near a year. She had never said anything about coming home. He wished he could go to Idaho to see her, but he knew he couldn't. It would cost too much. Then a thought struck him, and he slapped his hip and exclaimed aloud, "I bet I can!" If he could sell Samson, he could buy himself a ticket. Samson was getting big and handsome. He loved Sammy Thax and butted him playfully and let him ride him bareback around the barnyard. Sammy Thax would hate to let him go, but it was the only way he could think of to raise enough money to get to Idaho and back.

When he got home, his mother and Hester and Susan were all seated on the cool back porch, stoning cherries for preserves. His mother said, "Howdy, Sam. Get you some cherry pie out of the pantry if you want it, and after you rest a little, go bring us some fresh water from the spring. Looks like I stay thirsty on a day like this."

Sammy Thax tossed his books onto the broad bench near the kitchen door, went to the pantry, and got a slice of pie. When he finished eating it, he sat down on the back porch steps to rest. He heard his mother say to the girls, "Law, to think of Minnie settin' out to remarry so soon. I call it scandalous."

"Well, I don't, Ma," said Susan stoutly. "Uncle Clem has been dead nearly a year. Aunt Min needs a husband to help raise all her children."

"She's got Gran there to help with 'em," her mother answered. "Gran is a sight more help with children than most men would be."

"I don't guess the man has asked her yet," said Hester. "He might never ask her. So you don't need to fret, Ma."

Sammy Thax had been listening intently, but at first he didn't let on. Finally he said, "Who is Aunt Min's feller?"

Hester raised her eyebrows and said, "Little pitchers have big ears. Sam, didn't you know that curiosity killed a cat?"

"Why shouldn't Sam know that Aunt Min has got a beau?" asked Susan. "It's no disgrace. Read him Gran's letter, Ma. Sam thinks a heap of Gran."

Frowning a little, Mrs. Milliken reached into

her apron pocket and drew out a rather crumpled letter. Smoothing it on her knee, she unfolded it and began to read:

Dear Son, Daughter, and Family:
I am very well and hope this finds you all the same. Am glad spring has come. Have had enough of winter snow and ice. I guess the cherries is ripe down there and Early Harvest apples coming in. We don't have any fruit trees around here. Wheat is the main crop and potatoes second. Minnie's children is growing fast and nice behaved. Minnie is glad school is nearly out. She is wore out. I guess teaching all ages in a one room school is hard work. She has been keeping company lately with a widower. He is a nice man named Mr. Honiker with several children. His folks come here from Sweden. He farms. Sugar beets. I guess Sammy has growed a lot. I took his picture out of the album. Minnie got me a nice frame for it. I keep it on my bureau where I can see it more. It is a good likeness. Tell Sammy I'm glad Domino and Samson has lived and growed well.
I know he takes good care of them. He loves animals. Tell Hester I used some of that tatting she sent me to trim a lilac penang dress I made for

Sunday. It looks nice. Tell Susan I sleep regular on my nice pillow slips she sent me. They put me in mind of home. The ham and preserves and jam was awful good, all enjoyed them. Tell Sammy I keep my cedar limb in the clothes closet and it still smells good. Hope all stays well and crops is good this year. Regards to Rindy and Ella Lou and their family also the neighbors.

Love to all,
Gran

Sammy Thax's face was shining. He sprang to his feet and came and looked at the letter over his mother's shoulder. He said, "If Aunt Min marries, Gran might come home."

"Now don't set your heart on any such a thing," his mother said, folding the letter and returning it to her pocket. "I reckon we ought not to of mentioned getting any letter from Gran, if you are goin' to get all wrought up about her comin' home. Go fetch the water now."

Sammy Thax said no more. He took the water bucket and went to the springhouse. Once Sammy's father had said to his mother, "You always throw a wet blanket on folks' hopes." It was true.

In the days that followed he kept hoping they would get another letter from Gran, saying Aunt Min had married. But the days slid into weeks, and he heard no more about it.

His birthday was the end of June, and as the day approached, Sammy Thax missed Gran more than usual. She always had a gift for him, a knitted cap or gloves, a new Sunday shirt with tucks put in by hand, once a New Testament with his name printed on it in gold letters. And she always made him a cake with thick caramel icing on it, his favorite kind. Remembering all that, he crossed the hall and went into her room for the first time since she left. Her rocker stood near the window where she loved to sit and look out at the front yard and watch the birds that nested in the sugar maple tree. Dust lay thick on her bureau and little sewing table and the floor, but everything was in order. The room smelled musty though, and he raised the window and let the breeze blow through it.

The next morning he went fishing with Jud. When he got home, he found the downstairs empty. But upstairs his mother, Hester, and Susan were busy as bees, cleaning house. Susan was washing Gran's window, Hester was rubbing her bureau with beeswax. A wild hope made his heart thump. "Is

Gran comin' home?" he asked them. "Whatever made you think so?" asked Susan. "We've cleaned all the rest of the house, attic to cellar. We thought it was time to clean Gran's room." Sammy Thax's face fell. He went downstairs and called Bowser and made his way to the barn where his father was working on the mowing machine. He said abruptly, "Pa, can I sell Samson?"

His father turned in surprise. "Well, he's your calf, son," he said. "But he would bring you a better price six months from now. Cattle is awful cheap now, and he is too young to sell good. Why do you want to sell him? You think a heap of him, don't you?"

"Yessir, I do," Sammy Thax answered, "but I want to go see Gran. If I sold him, I could buy me a ticket is what I thought."

"Well, now," Mr. Milliken said, then hesitated, then went on, "we will have to think that over a while and talk to your Ma about it."

Sammy Thax turned away, discouraged. "Ma won't never agree to it," he thought.

Saturday morning came, and so did Sammy Thax's birthday. After a big birthday breakfast of fried chicken and stewed apples, Sammy's father had him sit down on the back porch for a haircut. With a towel tucked around Sammy's neck, Mr. Milliken trimmed away.

"Son, I think I'll take you and the girls to Richfield," said Mr. Milliken. "Being it's your birthday, you can have a soda at Mehaffey's Soda Fountain while I'm talking to Mr. Short at the courthouse about the rise in tax." He continued, "Confound it, it costs too much to live nowadays."

Everybody was bustling around, getting ready to go to town, except his mother, who rarely went anywhere. Hester and Susan were twirling and parading through the house with their new white pique dresses on. Even his father wore a starched white shirt and his black alpaca suit, like he did on Sunday preaching day.

"Hurry, Sammy, and dress," his mother said. "Pa says you are goin' to get a present." Sammy Thax looked at his mother, hard at work in the kitchen, and felt sorry for her. "Why don't you go, too, Ma?" he asked. "I'd best stay here and mind the house," she answered. "And I've got plenty to do."

"You don't never get to go anywhere, Ma," he said. "Don't you never get tired of working?" His mother laughed a short laugh and patted his shoulder. "Never mind," she said, "hard work never hurt anybody yet."

On the way to town in the surrey, Sammy Thax and his father rode on the front seat. Susan and Hester rode in the back. Sammy Thax could hear them whispering and giggling back there, talking as usual, he thought, about their beaux. His father didn't have much to say, but he looked more cheerful than usual, and now and then he whistled a tune.

When they got to the edge of town, instead of turning toward the courthouse on the square, where they usually hitched the team, Mr. Milliken turned down Green Street. Sammy Thax glanced up at him in surprise. All of a sudden Mr. Milliken put a hand behind his left ear and said, "Sam, what was that I heard?"

"A train whistle at the tunnel, Pa," said Sammy Thax. He felt out of breath and sort of scared. What if his father put him on the train to go to Idaho? The train rounded the curve and came in sight, its whistle blowing shrilly for the crossing. Hester clapped her hands over Sammy Thax's eyes and said, "Don't look yet, Sam." When the train stopped, she let him go. Sammy Thax sat still, feeling dazed. He blinked when he saw his grandmother at the top of the train steps, clutching her pocketbook and a satchel. The conductor helped her down the steps, and Sammy Thax scrambled off the wagon and grabbed her and knocked her flowered bonnet off.

143

"Sammy, bless your bones," said Gran. "Land sakes, how you have growed." Sammy Thax drew a long breath, threw back his shoulders, and stood straight and tall. He was grinning from ear to ear, and no wonder—he was the happiest boy in the state of Tennessee.